THE
DELIVERER

KWABENA ANKOMAH-KWAKYE

Sub Saharan Publishers

First published in Ghana, 2011 by
SUB-SAHARAN PUBLISHERS
P. O. BOX LG358
LEGON, ACCRA, GHANA
Email: saharanp@africaonline.com.gh

ISBN: 978-9988-647-75-9

DISCLAIMER
This story is entirely fictitious and any semblance to any persons or places is entirely coincidental.

Typesetting by Kwabena Agyepong
Cover design by Elkanah Kwadwo Mpesum

THE
DELIVERER

Dedicated to the voice that urges me on whenever the going gets tough in life, the heart that wishes blessings for me.

*The man of greatest strength is also
one of gentleness.
The most accomplished man learns both
from failure as well as success.
The man of strongest leadership knows how
to follow too – and that asking for help can
sometimes be the best thing he can do...
The wisest man of all is one
who takes a look within –
To embrace what he's becoming,
and to learn from where he's been.
If a man attempts all this,
Then he truly has the heart and soul
it takes to be a man.*

-anonymous

Some say our ancestors emerged from
a mysterious hole somewhere in
the Brong Ahafo Region of Ghana.
Others say they fell from the sky on
one rainy night, a few years after the second
battle of the gods.
Yet others say they were brought to our present
home through a mighty whirlwind.
The truth about our origin, I now believe
is buried so deep and so forever
that no man alive can dig it up.
My name is Osei Tutu,
only son of Yaa Mansa Badua...

.....and this is my story.

Chapter

Slowly, the procession marched into the forbidden Musuo Forest in the cool of the Friday evening. Another cloud was just preparing to hide the sun yet again. Dwellers of the night were preparing to come to life again with their distinctive cries and songs. Mother, sisters and friends form the tail of the procession, wailing uncontrollably with hands folded over heads and bodies covered with dirt as a result of they themselves throwing their bodies on the ground. Preceding them was the queen mother of Adum and her advisors and some slaves, then some elders of the Oyoko royal family, then Kofi Badu, the unfortunate father with eyes red from palm-wine and a determined refusal to shed tears, clinging to his staff as four strong young men march in front of him carrying his sweet daughter Yaa Mansa Badua shoulder-high on a mat with her hands tied in front of her. A few yards ahead, the drummers sweat despite the cool breeze as they kept thumping grave rhythms on the mighty *fontomfroms* as the chief priest and his aids dance mysteriously at the head of the procession.

For three continuous days she had sobbed and wailed and cried her innocence out and yet the only creatures who believed her were her mother, sisters and seemingly the dark and shiny pairs of eyes that furrow into holes and burrows as the thundering and wailing file past. Up above, the heavens seemed to show their shame for the day by blanketing Adum and surrounding villages with thick black clouds for a greater part of the day. A wicked judgment is being meted out to the most beautiful maiden in Adum village.

"Oh heaven hear my cry and bail me out, bail your daughter out." Yet again, she started to sing the melodious heart splitting dirge, and the men carrying her even wished they could fight for her freedom and be her warriors. Her sweet vibrating voice of desperation echoed so deep into the forest as into the hearts around. Perhaps except the hearts of the chief priest and the king's first wife who were the schemers of this.

When they got to the mighty *Odum* tree, the alter of the gods of Adum, the men lowered her into the grass. The chief priest slashed off the head of a black cock and spilled the blood on her feet. He chanted the banishment vows as Yaa hummed her dirge quietly. Her mother and well wishers wailed uncontrollably as others tried to restrain the women. The men tied Yaa to hooks on the stem of the tree. Her frail body shook gently as tears rolled down her cheeks, over the talisman around her neck and down her body. Slowly the procession began to return to the village, each person casting a final glance at the unfortunate beautiful girl.

Three months earlier, she had been chosen as the king's second wife because the king's first wife was unable to bear him a son. Even though she was very much in love with Kusi the hunter, she had no choice but to accept the king's proposal if they were to be counted among the living in Adum. She was out-doored as the second wife of Otumfuo Oti Akenten 1, king of Adum. In as much as the first wife and her aids tried to frustrate her, the King loved her more each day. Yaa was lovely and very respectful and she seemed to know exactly what the king wanted to be done at any particular time. The king's first wife got so jealous that she began to plan schemes upon schemes to get rid of Yaa, yet they all failed. She got the chief priest to side with her and together, they hatched the perfect plan that worked. They knew how Kusi the hunter still loved Yaa so they began spreading rumors that Yaa was flirting. The king got to hear of this and in as much as he did not want to believe it, he sent informers to monitor the movement of Yaa. When the king's first wife and the chief priest had gotten the feedback they wanted, they sent a messenger to inform Kusi that Yaa wanted to meet him under the neem tree on the way to the chief priest's village. Then another messenger was sent to inform Yaa that the chief priest wanted to see her at sunset. So that was how come Yaa was caught with Kusi under the neem tree at sunset, seemingly confirming the rumor. And when it came to light that Yaa had conceived, the unfortunate conclusion was drawn. In all the Asante villages, punishment for an unfaithful wife came in many forms. Over the years, they had varied a great deal. While some were brutal, others were fashioned merely to make mockery of the offending wife. In all cases the punishment was determined by the husband, but an unfaithful wife of the king received nothing less than banishment. And that was the reason why Yaa Mansa was sent as a sacrifice to the gods in *Musuo* Forest.

It had gotten pitch dark in the forest. The wind was whistling and howling so frightfully. Yaa was so scared she barely thought she was still alive. Then suddenly she began hearing strange sounds. She was not sure whether it was reality or her imagination. She began hearing loud noise of people laughing cunningly, sounds of howls and chants getting louder and louder. Her eyes widened as she fought for her sanity and life. Strange images began appearing to her and the frightening sounds were everywhere, all around. She struggled and screamed in desperation and then suddenly a hand reached from behind her and cupped her mouth... She fainted.

Back in the village, Kusi the hunter had vanished and everyone was in a sorrowful mood except of course, the King's first wife who was trying to hide her glee. Yaa's family had gathered around the fire in the compound as Kofi Badu, Yaa's father poured libation to bury the memory of his third daughter who was presumed to be no more. As the night wore on, the family began to retire to their mats one after the other until finally, all that remained on the compound were the embers from the fire. That night, the whole house slept in grief, from the man of the house to the goats in the pen, all the way down to the day old chicks. The flower that brought joy and pride to the house had been cruelly plucked and left in the rain to rot. Much as Kofi Badu tried to drown himself in palm wine, the memory of his precious daughter refused to let go of his mind. He tossed and turned and tossed and turned as he lay on his bamboo bed. He had won respect again when his daughter was chosen as the wife of the king. Hither to every body thought him a half-man because he came to this world to give birth to only daughters. What annoyed the elders of his family most was his blunt refusal to take a second wife. Every man in Adum thought him a fool for being stuck to a single woman in the name of love. To others, Ama's mother must surely have tied him up to a stake in *Antoa* (a renowned fetish).

Chapter

Slowly, she opened her eyes and took in her surroundings. She was lying on a raised mat with a towel soaked with warm water over her head. She stared back into the pair of wrinkled eyes that beamed into her face. She tried to recollect what had happened. Was she in *'Asamando'* (the land of the dead)? She opened her mouth to speak and the old man by her side motioned for her to keep quiet and lie still. He walked out of the hut and returned followed by a young man with a bowl of *"nnuhuu"*, (Asante food prepared by mashing soft cocoyam and adding palm nut soup.) He set the food on a small table next to the mat. Together, they helped her up, washed her face and mouth. When they sought to feed her, Yaa refused to eat unless she was told where she was and who they were. The old man was Opanin Asamoah and the young man was his son Bonsu. They explained that they had found her unconscious in the bushes on the path to their farm that morning and had taken her in. After eating, she told them who she was and all that had happened and the fact that she was even pregnant. Since she had no family now, she settled with Opanin Asamoah and Bonsu, his son in their village, Bantama. One thing was clear, no one knew who rescued her from the forbidden forest and dumped her where she was found. They lived happily together. Yaa cooked and made clothes for them. Eventually, it was time for Yaa to give birth to the baby.

There was a great storm the night she went into labour so there was no way help could be sought from the surrounding villages. The men had no choice but to deliver the baby themselves. They did it to the best of their knowledge but Yaa started bleeding profusely immediately after delivery. Even though they tried so hard to stop the bleeding, by morning the young woman had given up the ghost. Sorrow gripped Opanin and Bonsu as they held the delicate baby boy without a mother in their arms, an Adum prince in the house of peasant farmers. On the seventh day, after pouring libation to thank the gods for the gift and to the memory of the mother who never saw her son, Opanin Asamoah lifted the baby to *'Tweduampon Nyankopon'* (Almighty God) and to *'Asaase Yaa'* (mother earth) and named him Osei Tutu.

The year was about three hundred years before the coming of the white man. Those were the days when tribesmen and women, young and old, were all governed by kings, customs and rules, when men bought and sold their fellowmen as slaves, when clans and tribes fought to subdue rivals and weaker tribes.

Asante was a tribe made up of eighteen fragmented villages who where not united. Adum, Amakom, Manhyia, Bantama, Bohyen, Adansi and many others. The mighty Denkyira was a kingdom to the south of Asante. Denkyira had conquered the entire Asante villages one after the other and so they all paid tribute in the form of gold, farm produce and slaves to Denkyira at the beginning of every year. There had been a prophecy that the first son of the

Otumfuo would be the deliverer of Asante from Denkyira. A few months after the death of Yaa Mansa Badua, Otumfuo Oti Akenten's first wife had borne him a son with the help of the chief priest. Everybody hailed the little Kojo Akenten, the son of the Otumfuo's first wife as the Deliverer. A great celebration unlike any seen before in Asante was held to mark the naming ceremony of the Otumfuo's son. The king's wife dressed in full regalia and walked proudly for being the mother of the Deliverer out of the many wives of the Otumfuo.

Osei Tutu had grown to be four years old. He could pronounce every word in the Asante language and yet to the disappointment of Bonsu, his foster father, he could not stand much less walk. Opanin Asamoah had passed away months before. Bonsu had married a young woman from Bantama and had had children with her. At nine years, Osei Tutu was still crawling, unable to walk, and Bonsu always punished his children whenever he heard them making fun of Osei Tutu. Osei Tutu, could do everything like any normal child but to walk. Bonsu had made several sacrifices to the gods on Osei Tutu's behalf and yet there seemed to be no strength in his legs. Osei had been made to drink potions upon potions but all to no avail. Week after week, he was subjected to the torture of having one bitter herbal preparation after another forced down his throat. Bonsu carried him to rivers that were acclaimed to possess healing powers, both far and near. There were days poor Osei would be made to hang in a river so the water would flow over him for hours with the hope of giving him strength to walk. Night after night, Osei prayed to the gods for strength to walk even if not to run. He felt sorry for the hardship he felt he was putting Bonsu through. Bonsu was a very hardworking farmer, but because of the many treatments and herbalists he had to pay for Osei, he was almost always poor. A large part of the farm produce and animals he reared went away as gifts and payments to fetish priests and herbalists who gave him the promise that they would heal Osei. Month after month, all the outcome of his hard work went down the drain. This made Bonsu's wife grow bitter and bitter as seasons came and went with no improvement in their lives. Moreover, Osei on whom their sweat was being spent could not even contribute meaningfully to the work. Even though she did not harbour hatred for Osei, she only wished that her husband would come to the conclusion that enough had been done and spent. As each day passed, she got fed-up and started complaining; yet Bonsu would hear none of her arguments. Many a dawn, when all the household was asleep, Osei would hear his foster-parents arguing about his situation and the poverty into which he has plunged them. In as much as he loved his family, he felt he was a curse on them and began to lose hope that he would ever walk. During one of such dawn fights when he was ten years old, he plotted to do something that would bring a solution to his family's plight.

But how far could he go crawling on the ground?...every soul in the village knew him as Bonsu's cripple, where could he hide? ...Wouldn't his plot bring more pain to Bonsu, his Papa? Even as he pondered over this, he resolved. He had to run away.

Chapter 3

He appeared at the bank of the river, drenched in sweat and dirt. Behind him, he had left a very conspicuous trail as he crawled through the bushes. Even a five year old child would notice that 'a large animal' had been dragged through the bushes. He sat panting heavily and looked behind, staring at the new path he had created. Then he looked at the new nemesis he had to confront: the river. How was he going to cross to the other side? If he wanted to avoid the market, the traders and the farms, the only way out of Bantama village was to cross the river. Why didn't he think of this as he planned his runaway? He decided to rest a while and let ideas pour into his mind.

"Where there is a will, there will surely be a way." He said to himself.

He untied the sack from his aching back. The sack was made of palm leaves twisted and woven together. It was usually used to carry foodstuffs from the farms. Osei untied the mouth of the sack to reveal its contents. He had been saving for his journey for weeks. Inside his sack were eight roasted pieces of cocoyam, a cob of roasted corn, and a small knife wrapped in leaves. He figured out that he really underestimated the weight of his load for he was already weary even though he had hardly left the boundary of the village. A sudden churn in his stomach surfaced upon the sight of the roasted corn. Osei managed to convince himself of the abundance of food in the sack so he proceeded to take a few bites at the corn. In a matter of minutes, the whole cob of corn was gone! He dragged himself against a large *wawa* tree to rest. He began thinking about the few friends he would miss. Even though they were always complaining that he could not contribute to games that involved running, he mostly managed to convince them to play games in which he could effectively participate. Sometimes he felt sad when on the playground, he always ended up being the last one to be picked for a side. There were even times no side wanted to accept him. On one of those sad days, it became an open argument for the leaders of the groups. That day he really felt like a burden. He turned and crawled away home as the argument raged on only for his friends to pause and realise he had disappeared. He stared at the playground from behind their window, hoping his friends would feel sorry and send him an invitation to play again but it never came. They only went back to their game when they realised he had gone home. Sadly no one really seemed to need him. His only hope was his Papa, who still held on that he would walk one day. He missed his five younger brothers and sisters. Well, now he was going away so no one would be forced to either be nice to him or fetch water for him to bathe. The grass under the wawa tree seemed soft and cozy, so he lay down and continued in his thoughts.

....all his friends were standing submissively around him, behind them were his family and all the villagers, including the elders. There he was, standing! Talking to them that he was going to a far land ... they were all quiet as they beheld his glory, then he turned and was beginning to walk away...

"Osei!" "Wake up!" "What are you doing on this part of the riverside?" He woke from his slumber to behold the anger in his Papa, Bonsu's face.

"Answer me! Huh?"

In his rage, if it was not that Osei was a cripple, Bonsu might have tied him up and dragged him home behind him but instead, he lifted him and slung him across his shoulders with his numb limbs hanging on one side and his big head on the other. He marched through the centre of the village like a hunter returning from a hunt with deer slung across the shoulder. As they passed through the village square, Osei prayed the ground should open and swallow him up. The entire village seemed to know what he was about. Along the streets, women stood akimbo staring at him slung on the back of Bonsu with his sack being dragged along. Even the babies being carried on the backs of their mothers wanted to catch a glimpse of the cripple who decided to run away from the village. Each time someone managed to ask Bonsu where he found Osei, the shameful situation worsened. Bonsu would vent his anger with such venom that the pain became unbearable. Tears streamed down Osei's face. Then they would turn to look at Osei and ask, "Osei, where did you think you were going?", as if they cared so much. At long last they reached their collection of mud huts. Bonsu off-loaded him right in the center of the courtyard and then the grilling began. Peering over the short wall were his friends and the nosy villagers. Out of love, he was lashed. Quite severely.

The weeks went by and in as much as Osei wanted the episode

to be forgotten and erased out of memory, ever so often, a neighbour would visit Bonsu and would raise the issue and they will laugh over it. Many at times, Osei's friends would tease him and ask when he would attempt the next journey.

As Osei Tutu grew up, he seemed to be losing control of his emotions more and more. He would pick up on any gesture from another as making fun of him and would be troubled so much. Sometimes he would get so angry he would begin to stammer even though he was not a stammerer. One of those fateful days when he couldn't take the mocking any longer, he lifted a sharp stone and was just about to hurl it at one of his friends when he heard a loud "Stop!" He spun around to see a strange looking peddler with an intense and deep meaning gaze staring at him. "Drop the stone, youngman!" He screamed. Osei dropped the stone gently on the ground when he realised that the man had no arms and his garments were torn to shreds. He was a frightful sight to behold. With his chest still heaving up and down with rage he turned to find his friends standing around looking ashamed.

"When you are born to kill an elephant, you don't go bruising your knees chasing rats!" The strange man said.

" I don't understand." Osei replied.

"Go back home, wait when your father comes, tell him what I've told you." Then the man turned and walked away with a very awkward gait. Osei just cast one last glance at his sheepish looking friends and crawled home. When his Papa came back home in the evening from the farm, he narrated all that had happened to him. Bonsu never said a word. He kept the meaning to himself and resolved to do whatever he could to get Osei healed.

On moonlit nights, when all the children gathered by the fireside to listen to *ananse* stories, he dreaded stories that involved cripples. Even when a story involved laughter, Osei always felt the laughter was being directed at him and he felt bitter each day. He did not want anyone to laugh at him, he did not want anyone to pity him he even wanted no one to give him extra help. His Papa kept urging him day in and day out to channel the energy he wasted on being emotional into useful energy. He kept telling him; "To be angry is easy, but to be angry at the right person, at the right time, for the right reason, that is difficult." Though Osei could clearly understand the words, the real meaning of the statement was lost on him most of the time. He left the fireside with frustration and tears one night when the story required each child to take his or her turn dancing in the middle of the gathering to the drums. Knowing his plight, he kept shifting his place in the queue until it was obvious that he was the only one left who had not stepped forward to dance. In his bid for acceptance, he hopped onto the dance floor only to move his waist so awkwardly to the sound of the drumming that all burst into laughter, including the drummers. His Papa explained to him that if he wanted to regain respect among his peers, he should identify a skill and perfect it. The next morning, before going to the farm, Papa Bonsu carried Osei up to see the drum carver in a nearby village.

Even though he had a name, everyone in the surrounding Asante villages knew him as The Drum-maker. He was a queer old man with a perpetual smile etched on his face. He lived secluded with his six sons who were all renowned drummers. In those days, it was expected that one grew up to take up the trade of his father, uncle or in the case of girls, mother. The drum-makers as they were known had a long lineage of drummers so much that it was rumoured that their sons were born with elbows bent and palms stretched as if playing invisible drums. What was true was that from the inception of labour, they drum till the child was born. In that way, every child in their family entered the world to the sound of drumming.

After the customary exchange of greetings and drinking of water, Papa Bonsu went ahead to make known their reason for appearing at their village. Osei was delighted! Papa had brought him to live with the drum-maker for a full moon so he could learn to drum! The drum-maker was pleased to offer lessons to Osei because years before, Papa Bonsu and Opanin had rendered kind service to him. And so his training began. Osei loved to drum, besides he loved the idea that finally, there was something he could learn and be proud of even in his state. He practised in the morning, drummed in the afternoon, drummed in the evening, drummed at night, even drummed in his dreams! He drummed rain or shine. He drummed till the tip of his fingers flattened. He drummed till blisters formed in his palms. The drum-maker's sons loved him for his dedication. They even made a special drum he could play while sitting on the ground. So soon, his time was up and his Papa, who had missed him so much, came for him and they returned home to Bantama.

Even though Osei, gained the respect of his peers with his skills at drumming, he still yearned to be able to walk. To run around like all the other children in the village, to be able to farm and to hunt. One evening when he was thirteen years old, an incident happened that changed his life forever. As he sat under an odum tree carving a wooden doll for his younger sister, his foster mother, called out to him to come for his supper. Osei Tutu asked his sister to go and bring his food to him under the tree. Bonsu's wife got infuriated and started hurling insults at Osei Tutu. "Why doesn't your mother return from the grave to carry your food to you? You crippled bastard! She should have lived to endure the agony of seeing you thirteen years old and still crawling!" Osei Tutu's chest heaved up and down as tears welled in his eyes and anger swallowed him up. He cast a long glance towards the sky and with an unusual determination, got hold of the tree with one hand... and then another... He shut his eyes and suddenly, the whole compound had stood still watching Osei Tutu! Then slowly he pulled himself up unto his wobbly knees. Still clinging to the tree, he overcame the fear that he would fail and everybody around would laugh at him. He placed one foot on the ground and then another! His whole body was vibrating violently. Bonsu, who was by then returning from the farm, froze on seeing Osei Tutu, his boy, on his own two feet. "Come my boy, come to me. I know you can do it." He hissed. Osei Tutu slowly let go of the tree and took one wobbly step, stabled himself, then another, then another, "Papa, I'm walking! Papa, I'm walking!" he cried in tears, he collapsed into Bonsu's arms as they both wept for joy. From that day, the flame of hope was lit in the lives of Bonsu and Osei, his boy. He made a walking stick for him and helped him practice walking properly every morning before he left for the farm and in the evening when he returned. With a lot of determination, Osei began to walk on his own with the stick till the day he finally overcame his predicament and walked on his own without any help.

Chapter 4

At age sixteen, he was the most skilful hunter in his village. He had grown into a strong young man with skin as dark as charcoal. He had very bushy eyebrows and large eyeballs which made him look wiser and older than he really was. These in addition to his thick black Asante lips made him look fearful when he was filled with anger. Around his neck he wore a talisman nobody could discern, nor interpret its meaning. It was made from some dark hard unknown substance. His mother, Yaa Mansa was wearing it when she was found unconscious and so after her death, Opanin Asamoah had thought it wise to pass it down to young Osei when he came of age. With his bow and arrow, Osei exerted so much power and speed that he was not only a hunter but a warrior in the making. His Papa had noticed this and was trying to hide him from being enlisted into the army. In those days, it was an offence for a young man to refuse to serve in the army when chosen. As the days went by, he grew in wisdom and bravery and was finally working on controlling his emotions and building a good and cheerful nature.

Back in Adum, Kojo Akenten, the son of the first wife of the King, had also grown to be a very handsome young man with delicate facial features of a woman* but filled with dirty pride. By the King's decree, everyone bowed and called out "Deliverer" when he passed by. He was given the best of teachers to instruct him on Asante traditions and customs. As part of his twentieth birthday festivities, Kojo, went hunting with his aides. Osei, who had been in the forest hunting for three whole nights without game, happened to have strayed into that part of the forest. Although he had strayed further than where he normally hunted, he feared not because he knew his way back to his village. Since morning, Kojo had missed every single animal he had aimed at. He had changed so many bows that his aides needed to go back to Adum and bring new ones. Every time he missed and asked for a new bow, his aides bit their lips to refrain from laughing at their 'Deliverer'. Finally, here was one grasscutter he was going to kill to redeem his fallen pride. He took aim and just when he was about to release his arrow, the animal fell dead. Like lightening, an arrow from somewhere had pierced it right in between its eyes. The group all looked toward the direction from which arrow flew. Osei stood there with his bow in hand and a smile on his face. Suddenly, his smile disappeared when it dawned on him what he had done but he refused to run away. He stood still as Kojo ordered his guards to arrest him. Osei was made to kneel as Kojo breathed down his face.

"What you just did is the greatest insult to the Deliverer of Asante."

"Your majesty, I am only a hunter who wanted to kill game for my family. I never intended to interfere with your sport." Osei Tutu replied.

"Moron! Tie him up and bring him along!" Kojo Akenten ordered.

Chapter 5

Osei found himself locked up in a filthy prison in Adum with an empty stomach. His only crime was in finding meat for his family. What worried him most was the sorrow that he presumed was going through his Papa. He just wished he could send someone to tell his Papa he was neither dead nor lost. His first night as a prisoner was one of the toughest for him. He tossed and turned the whole night. Something strong inside kept telling him he was never meant to be a prisoner ever in his life. He thought of Bantama village with its beautiful trees and dried grass in the harmattan. The smell of burning bushes as farmers cleared their lands and burnt the weeds. He thought about his Papa and mother and little brothers and sisters and so much wished the 'Deliverer' would pardon and set him free. He missed Bantama village, with its nosy village folk. His mind wandered back to his childhood, when due to his ailment, he mostly spent his afternoons alone while the grown-ups with children of his age group all toiled on the farms. It was on one of such afternoons that he attempted his infamous escape. On his way to the river that day, he met three villagers who knew him well, when they asked him where he was headed to, he replied that he was on his way to fetch water by the riverside! With a loaded sack? Now he could smile about it but back then it didn't seem funny at all. As a matter of fact, it took not less than a whole year for his hatred for the villagers for turning him into a laughing stock subsided. Strangely, he had grown up to love them now. He was beginning to feel very restless.

Three months and still no word about Osei, his boy. Bonsu had consulted all the fetishes in Bantama. All confirmed that Osei was very much alive but none could point out his location. He took solace in the belief that Osei would one day return.

Messengers from Denkyira, (The mighty kingdom which ruled over Asante) known too well in Asante arrived yet again. The time of the year was up again when Denkyira sent messengers to collect tribute in the form of gold, produce and slaves from all the villages in Asante. In those days, slaves for Denkyira were selected from Asante prisoners and recalcitrant natives. Osei Tutu found himself en route to Denkyira on a Monday morning to face what destiny had for him. The way was long and dusty because of the dry season. His skin was cracking badly from long exposure in the sun without shea butter. And yet the caravan in front of him was filled with pots and bowls of shea butter from the northern states. He even pitied the slaves with cracking skin carrying the caravan filled with shea butter. It would take a very long time before he accepted that he was now a slave. At dusk, the group of messengers and slaves with caravans reached Fosu, the capital of Denkyira state. They were weary from walking all day from dawn. Fosu was the largest village most of them had ever seen. There were many huts grouped together into compounds by mud walls furnished with bright red clay. Lanes of foot beaten streets wove in between the various compounds. All the lanes seemed to converge infront of a huge palace; the Denkyira-hene's palace. 'So this is what all the gold and labour from Asante have been invested into' Osei Tutu thought to himself. None of the many Asante villages could boast of such an edifice. Even so, the thought never made him admire his homeland of Asante any less. Asante was his home, with its simple yet beautiful hills and greenery. The streams flowed gently across the landscape to nourish the farmlands. Denkyira may boast to be more developed but Asante with her natural beauty would never fade from his heart.

They were led to a part of the Denkyira-hene's palace where they were made to unload their goods. Most of the slaves had heard much of Denkyira but that was their first time of experiencing life in Denkyira. The citizens of Denkyira spoke a dialect of the Akan language but with a marked ascent. Many of the slaves including Osei Tutu were seeing Denkyira women for the first time and they could not take their eyes off them. In truth, they were more beautiful than Asante women; a rumour they had come to confirm for themselves. They were led to the slave quarters as many were murmuring why they were not allowed to wash off the dirt before being locked up. As if to shut them up the leader remarked that it was a taboo in Denkyira to bathe after sunset. They were locked up four in each cell. The stench and heat was unbearable because the cells were too small to accommodate the four. Osei Tutu introduced himself to the three men in his cell. They also took turns to introduce themselves. There was Kyei, the palm-wine taper, he was thrown into prison for poisoning a wine thief to death Then Aboagye, the carver; he killed his own wife and his friend for cheating on him. The third was Adjei, the royal kente weaver, his crime was refusing to address Kojo Akenten by the title 'the Deliverer' and he would tell nobody his reason for refusing to call when everyone was ordered to.

Osei Tutu's first day as a slave in Denkyira was all work. They worked from the break of dawn till setting sun in the royal farms. Like the first day, so were all the other days. They laboured in the farms throughout the day, breaking only for the day's meal when the sun was high up in the sky. After bathing in the evening before sunset, they gathered in the courtyard to relax. Some shared their dreams for their motherland Asante. Others talked about the past, their lives and their regrets. Osei sat alone most of the time listening to their stories and when he felt like he'd heard enough, he went to his cell and laid on his mat of straw. Osei Tutu grew in wisdom with each day he listened to the others and especially the time he spent with Adjei, the kente weaver. Adjei was a man in his late fifties, very calm and wise. He had deep set and discerning eyes. He came to like Osei Tutu very much and always shared a lot with him because he found Osei to be respectful and always ready to learn. The more time they spent together, the closer they became. From Adjei, Osei learned the meaning of most Asante symbols and their significance among other things. On one of those evenings, when the two were alone in the cell, Adjei who had noticed Osei Tutu's talisman and had been trying to find its meaning drew closer to Osei. He asked him what the significance of his talisman was. Osei looked down at it on his chest and shook his head. Adjei asked where he had it from and Osei told him his mother had it on her. One thing led to another and Osei went on to narrate all he knew about his past. Adjei, who had lived in Adum and knew the story of Yaa Mansa Badua, Osei's mother, took special interest in the boy from that evening onward.

Chapter 6

After a year as a slave in Denkyira, the Osei Tutu and the three who shared the same cell had developed close friendship and mutual respect. Through discipline, self-respect and hard work, he had come to be known as the slave who got things done the right way. It so happened that whenever Osei opened his mouth to speak, all the other slaves drew near to hear him even though he was far younger than most. All the slave supervisors had developed fondness for Osei Tutu although there were few of his fellow slaves who were jealous of Osei Tutu and Adjei kept an eye on Osei Tutu whenever they were near. As the fondness for Osei Tutu grew, so did the jealousy for him till something terrible happened one evening.

All the slaves were gathered in the courtyard that evening. Osei Tutu after listening to the stories chose to go and rest in his cell. After about an hour later, when Adjei and the others went into the cell, they met a horrific sight. Osei Tutu lay in a pool of blood! He had been stabbed in the rib on the way to his cell and had become unconscious. His face pale and body limp. Adjei quickly removed the leather strap around his waist and tied the wound to stop the bleeding. They lifted him over Kyei's shoulders and rushed him to the gates. After pleading with the guard, they rushed him to the local herbalist. The herbalist removed the leather strap and cleaned the wound with cassava sap as one of his assistants mashed some wild herbs. They covered wound with the herbs and tied it again with the leather strap. Adjei and the others stood around all that while sweating profusely in the cool breeze of the night. Osei still lay unconscious not even twitching an eyelid. After some time, the herbalist informed them that Osei had lost a lot of blood and so it would take some time for him to gain consciousness. They reluctantly left for the slave house. That night, none of Osei's friends slept a wink. They were all afraid that they might never have their young friend again.

Early the next morning, the herbalist prepared a potion and with the help of his assistants, he poured it in little drops down Osei's nostrils. His breathing began to improve and his pulse was evident. His friends received the news with much relief. After two days with the herbalist, Osei Tutu finally gained consciousness. An assistant by name Ama Birago offered to always be at his service even though the herbalist protested vehemently. This was because Ama Birago was a princess of Denkyira. And it was not proper for a princess to attend to a slave. She had turned twenty, two years younger than Osei. She had been brought to the herbalist to be trained in the ways of herbal preparations and healing. Initially, she saw healing Osei Tutu as a challenge of how well she could practice but as time went on she grew to like his mannerisms and attitude.

Ama was a very beautiful princess with long black hair plaited in braids. In as much as she was beautiful, Ama was strangely strong willed and a very determined young woman. From child hood she had proved more intelligent than her age mates. Ama was fond of listening to advice and wisdom from the old men and women in the palace, unlike girls of her age. She was slender but had ample breasts and hips that made men stare at her and made her shy most of the time. There seemed to be no scratch on her with the exception of the tribal mark she wore beautifully on her right cheek. When she smiled, her white teeth matched with her pure white eyes and even the herbalist could not fail to notice the beauty in her. Like Osei Tutu, she had thick sensuous African lips. Osei could stare at her all day as she went about her training and sometimes even forgot he was meant to get healed and return to the slave-house. As a princess, she was always adorned with special beads around her neck, waist and wrists that never ceased to fascinate Osei. Whenever she caught him staring at her, she let go of that smile that seem to melt even the heart of the gods. When Osei was strong enough, she would ask him about Asante and about all the myths that she had heard. Osei would gladly tell her Asante stories and folklore. The six weeks he spent with the herbalist were the sweetest times in his entire life. Then one evening when they were alone, by the fire in the small yard, Ama asked him why he was a slave. Osei narrated all that had happened to him. He told her about Bonsu, his foster father and Opanin, the old man he never grew to see and all his brothers and sisters. She sobbed quietly as she listened to him. Her tears shone like polished ivory in the light of the flame. She gently reached out and touched his hand. She held it and placed his palm on her smooth cheeks and sobbed some more. Osei felt so much like hugging her close but the line of separation between them was very clear. She was a princess in her land and he, a slave in a foreign land. He cast his eyes down at that thought and feelings of escape sneaked into his mind but he quickly drove them away. From the tales he heard from the slave courtyard, not many slaves had made it out of Denkyira alive. He'd rather prefer to be stabbed thirty times so he could see Ama Birago always than to risk his life trying to escape. His palm was wet with tears from Ama's cheek resting in his palm. Then suddenly it occurred to him there wouldn't be more times like this because he was almost completely healed. He asked Ama how long the herbalist would allow him to stay. That broke new streams of tears. It was as if a spell had been cast on both of them. They felt like they could never live without each other ever again. None of them had ever fallen in love before. They had only heard love tales and yet what they felt for each other was so much like those in the tales. First loves who are miles apart in social status, tribe and culture. There was virtually no chance in a million that things could work out between them even though they had so much joy when there were together. The herbalist who had been watching them all that while decided it was enough. He moved closer to pick a stool so they would notice he was around. Ama got up and quickly hid her face from the light, she helped Osei Tutu up and walked him slowly to his hut. She whispered good night and went into her hut. Osei lay flat on his back. The pain at his side greatly reduced. He had never been able to free himself of the thought of home. If he was still in Bantama, his Papa would be looking for a maiden for him to marry by this age. Probably a maiden who was humble, faithful, skilled at smoking meat since he was destined to be a hunter and also not beautiful. He always disagreed with his Papa on the view that a hunter should not dream of marrying a beautiful girl. Papa gave the reason that since hunters barely spent nights at home, a beautiful wife home alone would only attract other men and eventually would be unfaithful. Unfortunately, he had done the exact opposite. Not only had he fallen for a beautiful girl, who was out-spoken, had never smoked meat in her life before, he had fallen in love with a woman he would never see again after he is sent back to the slave-house, much less dream of marrying. He shut his eyes and tried to sleep his sorrows away.

Three huts away, Ama lay on her mat eyes wide awake trying to find a way of getting Osei to stay with her in the palace even if not for a lifetime. She had even overstayed at the herbalist's place. Her training was over. She was just there because she wanted to know more and she loved to work with the affable herbalist. Then an idea surfaced in her mind.

Back in the cell, Adjei and the others couldn't wait to have their young friend back. If only they were free men, they could have visited him every day. No matter how much they listened and searched, they couldn't find the one who stabbed Osei. Osei himself never saw who it was, making it dangerous for Osei to ever walk around the slave-house alone.

Ama woke up early the next morning and with her escort, went to the palace to see her mother. She told her about her last days with the herbalist and about an intelligent and hardworking Asante slave who was stabbed in the slave-house. She pleaded with her mother to allow Osei to move into the quarters in the palace and serve them. Initially, her mother was against her request because she saw some degree of self-interest in her daughter's request and didn't understand why she should be so worried about one Asante slave out of the hundreds of slaves in Denkyira. Finally she gave in to her daughter's request because she wanted to meet this Osei Tutu and see things for herself. She informed the chief-servant and they arranged with the head of the slave-guard to move Osei into the palace. When Osei's friends heard he would be joining them no more, they were sad but they later reasoned that was the only way to ensure his safety.

Chapter 7

Osei moved to the palace when he was completely healed. As the princess wished, he was assigned to cleaning the palace and helping with any manual work. The food here was far better than what he used to eat in the slave-house and they even ate from wooden bowls unlike the plantain leaves from which all the slaves ate their food back in the slave-house. In as much as he cherished the Asante way of life he had been brought up , each day in Denkyira palace lured him to embrace this new land. Especially their staple food. The denkyira women would boil cassava and plantain and would pound them together till they formed a very uniform paste which they served with soup. He really enjoyed this particular food yet he held firm the love of his native land in his heart.

Osei was asked to work under a very old servant named Oduro. As was his nature, he worked diligently and above what was even expected of him. He would wake up very early before most of the other slaves woke up and then start bringing in the fire wood needed to cook the food for the palace. The other slaves would join in when they woke up. After they had brought in enough, they would be assigned large troughs to fill with water. Slaves in the palace were normally natives of Denkyira and foreign slaves who had no reason of escaping. They were not guarded so much like those in the slave-house. After filling the troughs, they would sweep the whole compound. Then they were allowed to take their baths and prepare their own food. After eating, they would then be assigned their work for the day. It could be going to the farms to bring in the produce or joining the royal hunters to kill game. Sometimes too they removed the husks from corn and milled the corn. That was one of the most tedious works in the palace. After removing the husks from a mountain of corn, one's palm would be filled with blisters and blood. Whenever they went to bring in the farm produce, Osei met his friends and they talked about how things were going on in each other's life. Even though life as a palace slave was the dream of many slaves, Osei still wished to be a free man. Most of his afternoons were spent with Ama. They talked about love when they were out of earshot from the others and immediately changed to talk about food or festivals when they noticed any other person getting nearer. Although they both knew there was nowhere for them to go, they still loved the adventure of trying to fall in love. They shared dreams of building a home together although they both knew it would never happen. They talked of their future children and gave them names. Ama was fascinated by the meaning of the Asante names and she would listen to Osei as he told her about funny names and their meanings. Names like Yaw Ponkor literally translated as "Yaw Horse" would be given to a boy born on Thursday because one of his ancestors was a very fast runner. Another would be Kwaku Bonsam, literally translated as "Kwaku Devil!". Ama would laugh so hard that she would almost choke on her laughter. On other days, he would share jokes with her in whispers because it was not allowed for Denkyira throne heirs and heiresses to share jokes nor listen to them. Ama had a good chance to be a queen in Denkyira because she was the only daughter of the present Denkyira-hene and the first daughter in their lineage. She mixed up with most of the other slaves so it would not seem there was something going on between Osei and her. At other times too, in the cool of the evening, when they were alone, they would touch each other on the arms and stroke their cheeks. They would both shed tears and wished situations were different. Ama never stayed in the slave-quarters after the evening meal. She would be reprimanded for being outside the main house of the palace after night fall. Deep inside, she knew she loved Osei Tutu and she couldn't help but see him everyday but she still wanted more although that was impossible. Running away for love had crossed through Osei's mind over a hundred times but he knew they wouldn't go far before they were caught. All the warriors in Denkyira would be tasked to search for them. Even though he knew he was a good hunter, this was a foreign land and the natives knew the terrain like the back of their hands. Suddenly things were getting out of hand. On the nights when all the subjects would be summoned before the King, Ama and Osei would be winking at each other at the meeting and then sneak out of sight of the others, they would tickle each other and giggle. They would hug and stroke their faces and arms. When they hear the linguist giving the final address, they would quickly mix up with the rest. When their eyes met again, they would make faces at each other.

It had gotten to the time of the year when a hunting competition was organised for Denkyira royals. The men from each of the royal families went into the nearby forest to hunt for deer. Osei was chosen as one of the aides to a prince who was a general in a division of the Denkyira army. He carried the hunting tools and water meant for the prince. The sun was up and it was a great day for hunting. This brought back memories to Osei; why he became a slave. Although the prince was very friendly, Osei was sad and couldn't contribute much to the conversation as they hunted. The first day ended with a fairly good catch. Somehow, he liked Osei for his service and asked him to go along with him the next day. The next morning, the prince sent an aid to call Osei before the departure time. He asked him what was bothering him the day before and Osei told him how he became a slave. When he got to know Osei was a hunter, he asked him to hunt along with him although Osei was reluctant. That day saw them making more catch than all the other men who went out to hunt. They had to even leave some of the game in the bush to be later collected by the other aides. By the end of the third and final day, the prince had won the prize at stake. He called Osei into his room and gave him gold nuggets as a reward. Osei humbly refused to accept the reward and that made the prince like him even more. They became friends from that day onwards. Whenever Osei was free from his chores, he would ask for permission from the head of the palace slaves and would go to the prince in another part of the palace. He would ask him questions on how it was that one man could lead a multitude into battle. The prince took his time and taught him all about leading an army and the techniques of battle. Osei eagerly learned all the general taught him each day. When he went to bed, he would imagine himself leading a group of men and directing them on how to combat their enemy. He thus never forgot all he learned. His lessons ended when the prince was asked to lead his men into a battle with the Fante states to the south of Denkyira. Osei waited for months but the prince never returned from the battle.

On days that the palace slaves went to bring in the farm produce, even though he would be happy to see his friends, he also felt bad when he saw them sweating out in the grown weeds with bare backs under the extremely hot sun. He felt he had to do something to repay them for saving his life. Eventually, he hatched a plan to get them out of the common slave-house. He began talking about the beauty of Asante *kente* to Ama. Curious Ama had seen the queenmother wear some on special occasions. The making of Asante *kente* was a secret to a special family in an Asante village called Bonwire. The men of the family would bind yarns of thread around sticks, disappear into the bushes for months and would return with the *kente*. Adjei, the royal kente weaver hailed from that family. Osei pleaded with Ama to get Adjei to be housed in the palace to produce for her family. Although she feared her request would be rejected, she asked her mother out of love for Osei and the thrill of being clad in *kente*. Her mother had the task of presenting the idea to the queen. In Denkyira as in Asante and nearby Akan states, the queen was never the wife of the king. She was mostly the sister or aunt of the King. Finally it was agreed and Adjei was moved into the palace to be the royal kente weaver of Denkyira. He had Kyei and Aboagye brought into the palace to carve a weaving loom for him. That was how Osei managed to get all his friends to be made palace slaves. Adjei was so respected that he could hardly be called a slave. Since he claimed kente could never be woven in public, he was given a special room in which he lived and wove all his days. His food was brought to him by Osei and together, they ate and shared so many secrets. Adjei taught him many secrets and traditions of all the villages in Asante. After a few months, Adjei had become like a father to him. Osei felt he could not keep what was going on with Ama to himself any longer. He told Adjei one evening. Adjei got terrified because he knew what that could lead to. Even if nothing bad happened, he knew the consequences if Osei was caught with the Denkyira princess. He asked Osei to put an immediate end to seeing Ama Birago after sunset. Osei respected Adjei and made up his mind to heed the advice; yet doing what he had been told was another thing. Things with Ama rather became more intense till one day, and the unfortunate happened.

Chapter 8

Three years had passed so quickly. Osei was now a young man of twenty-five years. It was that time of the year when Denkyira was celebrating the Akwasidae festival. This was a week-long festive occasion to celebrate the end of a harvest season. There was a lot of merrymaking, drumming, dancing and drinking of sweet palm-wine. On a Thursday evening, most of the palace subjects were following the king as he was being paraded through the streets of Denkyira. Ama had arranged to meet Osei in an obscure part of the palace. Osei had waited for a long time but there was no sight of his love. Then he saw someone signalling at him. He drew nearer and found it was one of Ama's handmaids. She told him Ama wanted him to come to her room. She put a veil over Osei's head and led him through the women's quarters into the part of the palace allocated for the wives of the king. He entered Ama's room and found her weeping on her bed of straw. He stood looking round Ama's tidy room. The room was smeared with beautiful white clay that shone even in the candlelight. On her walls hung her articles, neatly arranged. She was a very civilised and well cultured young woman. Ama asked the maid to leave them alone. The sad news was that her father proposed a contest as part of the festivities and promised to give her hand in marriage to the winner. The winner was a cruel warrior she would never be happy with. At that moment, Osei started shaking all over, he had known all along this day would come and yet he felt he could prevent it. He held her tight and tried to comfort her. She kept on weeping so much Osei didn't know what to do. He held her head between his palms and looked into her eyes.

"Ama, ...Ama, I love you."

"You? You do?"

"Ye-yes, I do"

"Swear that you love me with all your heart."

"I swear by the memory of my mother whom I never met alive."

Ama could not believe her ears. Why had the world been so cruel to them? Why her? Why had her love appeared as a slave from a different tribe? She slowly removed the beads around her neck and untied the piece of cloth covering her bosom. Osei gasped at her beauty and the thought of what was about to happen. He knew they were going too far and yet he hadn't the will to stop it. "Osei learn to control your emotions. Never let your heart control your head." These words from Papa and also from Adjei kept ringing in his head and yet he felt helpless. He stepped backwards but Ama hang on to him. "I would rather you know me before the beast does." She whispered. Osei removed his smock and inner garments and together, they crossed the river of innocence. Half an hour later, they were lying in each other's arms unaware of what would be happening next. So many thoughts were going through each other's mind. They both knew they had done the most abominable thing ever to happen in Fosu and yet in a way they felt content and ready to defend their action. Then suddenly, they heard running footsteps outside the door. Men shouting and a woman screaming.

"Where is the room? Huh!" the man asked

"He....here...the one we just past" the woman answered crying.

Osei quickly rolled off the bed and hid under the bed as the man began pounding on the door. Ama blew off the lamp and plunged the room into darkness. She quickly tied on her clothes.

"Ah! Who is it?" she asked.

"Open the door princess. We have been ordered to search your room!"

There were three guards with a flame torch. They entered and looked around. From the look of fear on Ama's face, they knew something had gone on.

"Where is the Asante slave?" the leader demanded?

"What Asante slave?" Ama asked.

"Don't lie! You thought nobody saw you sneak the slave into your room." the man snapped back.

"He's left." Ama said in tears.

"You are to come with us." The man hissed as he dragged Ama out of the room. Osei's eyes widened in horror. He knew if he didn't find his way out of Denkyira, he would be a dead man before sunrise. He put on his smock and jumped out of the window not knowing exactly what to do. The palace was fully walled with guards standing at every ten metre interval. The gates were heavily guarded. His only hope lay in the fact that most of the guards were with the king's procession in the village centre. Luckily for him security at the palace had been reduced as a result. Crouching behind Ama's window, he could see all the palace slaves being led out of their rooms into the slave-yard. He knew if he were to make it out of Fosu, he needed to run fast before a search team was assembled. He ran in the shadows towards the eastern wall. He crouched whenever he heard or saw someone approaching. When he reached a section of the wall, there was no guard in sight. He jumped and held the top part of the wall, scratching his left palm on a spike. Just as he was about to roll his right leg over the wall, he felt the edge of a spear poke at his back.

"Fool, get down! You are a dead man!"

Osei awoke suddenly beside Ama. It had been a bad dream. She was staring straight into his face, her eyes, drenched with tears. She asked what it was that had woken him suddenly. They dressed up and he began narrating his nightmare to her, just then, they heard running footsteps outside the door. Men shouting and a woman screaming.

"Where is the room? Huh!" the man asked

"He....here...the one we just past" the woman answered crying.

Osei quickly rolled off the bed and hid under the bed as the man began pounding on the door. Ama blew off the lamp and plunged the room into darkness. She quickly tied on her clothes. Everything happened just as it was in the dream. Osei couldn't believe he had had a premonition. He crouched in the darkness behind a mango tree a few metres from the eastern wall. This time, the king had returned to the palace and so the guards had been doubled. Even then Osei resolved never to allow himself to be captured and tortured because he followed his heart. His eyes were red with tears and bewilderment. Just in front of the wall was a guard with a bow slung on his shoulder and another a few yards away. He gathered his wits and cast his mind to his hunting days. He crouched and moved slowly toward the guard, then like lightening he dived and struck him at the base of the neck. He let out a scream and Osei hit him hard at the base of the skull knocking him out cold. He picked up the bow and arrows just in time to see the second guard with a sword in hand charging towards him. He mounted an arrow in the bow and shot right into his heart. The guard choked and fell down backwards. Osei stood there trembling. He had never killed a man before. Now he knew there was no turning back. Even if his life would have been spared for defiling the throne of Denkyira, he would definitely not be allowed to live after killing a royal guard. He removed the guard's belt and footwear and wore them, with the sword, bow and arrows slung securely. He jumped and held the wall, this time, avoiding the spikes and threw his leg over the wall. He jumped and landed in a thicket on the other side. His arms and legs scratched with thorns. Beads of cold blood trickling from the cuts. He untied the sword and cut his way through the thicket. He had lost track of time and didn't seem to care about anything except for his life. Too many things were going through his mind at the same time for him to care about time. He soon came to a footpath. He looked left and right not knowing which one would lead him out of Fosu and Denkyira; and which one would take him right into the hands of his pursuers. He whispered his first prayer in a long time. He begged for forgiveness from the souls of his mother and ancestors he never knew. Why did he ignore the many warnings that were given by the wise Adjei? He should have heeded to wise counsel. Well, the unfortunate has already happened. What next? He chose to go right. He run as fast as he could and then began walking when he was tired. The sword at his side was quite heavy but he reasoned he might need it. He kept in the shadows and walked hurriedly on. Every time Ama's face came to his mind, his eyes got filled with tears. He loved her. He knew it and wished he had not even ventured entering her room. Not only had he endangered their lives but he had made the woman he loved a spectacle in the whole of Denkyira. Adjei warned him. Adjei did. He would run for a few minutes and then walk till he felt revived to run again. He could hear the cries of animals he knew so well, the meaning of their cries and their habits. He could even discern how far the animals were from how loud the cry was. Now he was a fugitive. Life had become bitter again all of a sudden. As all these thoughts run through his mind, he kept faith with the belief that his destiny pointed to greatness. Ever since he overcame his inability to walk during childhood, he had developed the strong believe that until he was no more, no situation nor circumstance was too grave to redeem or correct. Such positive thoughts filled him with hope, hope that made him journey on even though his bones and muscles were squealing with wear and tiredness. He ran on. Where he was headed to, he knew not, what he would meet in the next minute, he had no idea, he needed to get away to a land where he would be safe to build a life again. "Do not let your heart rule your head." It kept resounding in his ears. All living creatures around seemed to be whispering "You should have listened to wise counsel".

Chapter 9

Three nights and three days had passed since Osei ran away from Denkyira. Somewhere deep within, a voice kept whispering to him to head in the direction of the rising sun, and so he ran, he ran with all the strength left in him. He had barely eaten or drank anything. A handful of wild berries he picked up along the way during the second day was all he had had. Now he was both exhausted and very hungry. Up above, crows all with black feathers and a distinctive white patch glided and every now and then filled his ears with their cries. It was almost sunset and he had not come across a single soul much less a village. Was he being pursued? Had they picked his track? How far behind were they? These were questions that kept running through his mind and made him never willing to even pause for a much needed rest, yet a man could only run for so long without his muscles failing. He slumped under the shade of a guava tree a few yards off the path and unfastened the sword at his side. Around him, there was utter stillness with the only sign of life being the vast wild grass and the army of ants marching back to their mound a few yards away after the day's work. As he sat in the silence watching the glow of the sun as it went to sleep beyond the western hills, his mind kept going over the sequence of events that had him sitting in the middle of nowhere weak and hungry. Suddenly, there was a chirping sound, then a gradual movement that flowed through the grass to the left of the ant mound. The hunter that he was, his mind forgot all the tiredness that he felt, he drew the sword from the sheath and crouched low. Then he moved slowly but steadily in the direction of whatever was moving underneath the grass. Whatever it was, he could almost sense the smell of roasting bushmeat on a stove of naked fire back in Bantama and he yearned to make up for all the evenings he had spent through with an empty belly. As he got closer, it was also blindly groping towards him. Then he stopped and waited... three paces away he saw it, grasscutter! At that moment, it lifted its head and saw its worst enemy, a hunter! Osei dived! The grasscutter dashed! He smacked the ground with a heavy thud! He missed. Quickly he sprung up as the animal began weaving through the grass. He wasn't about to let this one go! The chase began! He sprinted after it as if his very life depended on catching it. The grasscutter made a few zig-zags to throw its pursuer off but to no avail then it decided to make the final dash for its hole within the roots of the very guava tree Osei came to sit under. It leapt hoping to land right inside the hole but that day wasn't a lucky day for it. It missed and struck right against the root by its hole! Within a twinkle, Osei had it by the neck. A small giggle of success escaped from his throat as his eyes beamed at the sight of the tasty grasscutter firmly within his grasp. It wriggled against him as he carried it to a flat rock. In his mind, he would slash the throat and then hang it for a while as the blood drained. After, he would empty the bowels onto large leaves and then would find dried grass, arrange them over a patch as he struck two rough stones against each other to spark a fire. Then he would roast the meat and satisfy his hunger. How he wished he had a piece of a tasty rock the Denkyiras called salt. He heard it was brought from the south where the people there mined it from the big river. In Asante, it was so expensive the village chiefs were the only ones who could afford it but in Denkyira, it was quite abundant. "Salt or no salt, he was going to make this grasscutter the best meal he had ever had." He thought. Osei held the front legs together with the head and turned the animal on its back... His heart sank.

The grasscutter had nipples lining its belly. It was a nursing mother. Osei sat staring at it for what seemed like hours, torn between mercy on the grasscutter and the hunger tearing at his stomach. Then he heard but couldn't believe it.

"Please have mercy and spare my life." Huh? The grasscutter was talking!

"I just had a litter of young ones seven days ago, if you kill me, they will all die from starvation and cold."

True to what the animal was saying, Osei looked at the hole and in there were several shiny pairs of dark brown eyes staring at him with an unsaid prayer of salvation for their mother. He was astonished. He had never met a talking grasscutter, only heard of animals talking in stories and folktales. Osei looked down at the animal and had pity. A hunter touched by the pleadings of a grasscutter. "What kind of a hunter would let an animal go because he thought he heard it begging for mercy?" He thought. Against reason and the norm of a hunter's trade, he let the grasscutter go. It quickly dashed for the hole, stopped at the entrance, cast one last long glance at the merciful hunter and disappeared down the hole with its young ones. Osei slept hungry yet again. Even with the hunger, he slept like a log.

Dawn came to find Osei very much asleep. Slowly he opened his eyes and took in his surroundings. Sharp pains from bruises he had sustained through his recent journey tore at him from every side. His eyes hurting from the rays of sun filtering through the leaves of the tree began to focus on something a little strange. At his feet laid a small bulging sack tied at the end with climbing plants. He tried recollecting but he could not remember ever noticing anything like that the evening before. Then he remembered the talking grasscutter. He glanced at the guava tree and sure enough there was the hole. He slowly untied the sack and inside were fruits! Fruits from every land, sweet smelling fresh fruits. Tangerines, lemons, mangoes, pear, coconut, pawpaw, and even fruits he never knew existed. His first instinct was to swallow the whole sack at a go but his mind went back to the strange grasscutter whose life he spared. He drew near the hole only to find it was gone! Along with all the litter. There was evidence of fur and broken twigs but no grasscutter. It dawned on him that the grasscutter was showing gratitude for his kindness.

"But how could a small grasscutter carry this weight of a sack?" He thought. He gave thanks, reached into the sack and started munching through the contents. Before long, his hand touched something unusual of a fruit. He pulled it out of the sack to find it was a dirty piece of cloth tied around a hard object. Out of curiosity, he put aside the piece of pawpaw he was eating and untied the cloth. Lo! He gasped at what he saw.

Wrapped in the piece of dirty cloth, was a small lump of gold! Pure gold!

"Ei!" He exclaimed! He sprang up, tied the knot to the sack of fruits, fastened his sword to his waist and continued on his journey to freedom. There seemed to be renewed energy in his steps after the encounter with the grasscutter. Through his kindness not only had he had enough food to eat, he was also a wealthy man. Plans kept pouring into his mind as he journeyed along. He would find a small village and settle down to be a farmer. He would buy farm slaves and build a huge farm and then probably find a nice young woman to marry. One who looked and had mannerisms like Ama. At the thought of Ama, a sudden sadness fell over him.

"What happened that night after he escaped? The disgrace? Would she go ahead and be another's wife?" He kept torturing himself until he heard it. That sound. The sound of a flowing stream. For a moment, it sounded too good to be true. He cut through the bushes as he made his way to the source of the sweet sound. True to his wishes, it was a fresh gently flowing stream.

"Ah!" he breathed a sigh of relief.

He got down on his knees and washed his face and hands. Then for what seemed like hours, he knelt there gulping down the water in mouthfuls. After drinking to his satisfaction, he rolled over and laid on his back, staring at the clear blue afternoon sky above the top of the trees. For once in a very long time, he felt at peace. There and then he decided to lay aside his troubled past and look to build a new life. What lay ahead of him troubled him almost as much as what he had left behind. He didn't know where he was or what laid in store for him. Was he still in the land of the Denkyiras? Was he being tracked? The thought suddenly startled him. He got on his feet and thought about where to go next. Should he turn and continue going eastwards or he should walk along the riverbanks. He chose the latter for two reasons: one stemming from the thirst he had to endure over an unknown land before the gods gifted him with this river and the other being that he stood a better chance of meeting a settlement along the river. Perhaps he could find a new dwelling amidst them. He followed the river downstream hoping it would not make him walk all day in circles. After walking for a greater part of the afternoon, he came across the first sign of a settlement. A small farm on the banks of the river. Getting closer, he realised the plants though looked like leaves of cocoyam were different. His years spent in Fosu as a farm-hand for the palace had brought him across a wide-range of foreign crops and fruits. Judging from the marshy nature of the terrain, he concluded that these were taros. Taros were much bigger than cocoyam and softer when cooked. Legend had it that it was forbidden in a certain village because the chief of that village choked on taros whiles eating and talking at the same time and died! Osei carefully navigated his way through the farm so as not to cause harm to a potential neighbour's hardwork.

After passing through more farms, he came across a path which led straight from the river. He concluded that the path probably linked the village to the stream. He followed the path until he came to an intersection that branched in four different directions. Which way should he go? As he stood there contemplating, three young boys came running past him on barefoot with a lot of excitement from one direction. Before he could stop them and inquire about where he was they were gone. Out of curiosity, he followed their direction hiding in the shadows the trees provided. A few yards ahead, he heard voices. The voices were those of two women having a conversation. Straining his ears, he realised they were speaking a language that was similar to Asante but some words were strange to his ears. After listening a while, he gathered enough courage and stepped out from behind the trees. He tried to look a little cheerful so as not to scare them, knowing very well how manly he looked. Back in Denkyira, Asante men were not considered handsome because they were mostly shorter and muscularly built. In addition they had large feet which seemed to spread like those of a duck as they walked. Not only that, but also the colour of their eyes were never as white as the Denkyiras. In fact, they were much closer to a shade of red than white! Osei was an exception when it came to height but he shared the other attributes with his tribesmen in addition to very thick eyebrows that seemed to touch each other when he was furious. As he approached them, he noticed one had on her head water in an earthenware pot and the other was carrying hers under her arm. Each wore plain pieces of coverings on their torso and from the waist to the knee and was barefooted. Unlike where he came from, their hair was neither braided nor combed. The two women were so engrossed in their conversation that they failed to see him coming towards them.

"Ei! Ntiamoah! It serves him right! Too much wisdom will cause a man to greet a goat!" The taller one exclaimed.

"Oh sister, don't be so mean. Ntiamoah doesn't deserve to die." The other remarked.

"Says who? I perfectly agree with the chief! As you make your bed, so you should be prepared to lie on it."

"Mm mm!" Osei cleared his throat and startled them. They looked him up and down slowly with their eyes in silence. The longer the silence, the more nervous he became so he proceeded and introduced himself as a hunter who had strayed into their part of the world.

Chapter 10

N Tiamoah was a wise man. For that everybody in Akyem village agreed. What most of the villagers hated was how he chose not to farm nor hunt nor weave nor carve to make a living. He made a living from his wisdom. Everyone thought him a lazy man yet he lived in much more abundance than most of his village folk who laboured all day in the bushes and farms. His was to appear at the village square, put forward an adage or a riddle and then dare his folks to find the meaning to the riddle for a handsome prize. Of course, he who dared had to pay a token of cowries or farm produce or whatever was acceptable. Over the years, Ntiamoah had built a life from that. Someone even staked his wife and son. Ntiamoah married the woman, Mansa and adopted the son when the man failed to find the answer to his riddle! The bitter man happened to be Okyere, the chief's younger brother. But that particular day Osei appeared in Akyem village, Ntiamoah was in hot waters!

Weeks before, Ntiamoah as usual appeared in the village square one fine Sunday evening in a strange haircut. He sported three distinct mounds on his head and promised to offer a piece of gold to anyone who found out the meaning of his haircut. Since it was harvest time, many men, some from the villages around Akyem staked. Weeks went by with no one succeeding in finding the meaning of Ntiamoah's haircut. Finally, the day he was to declare the answer approached with no one coming forward with any more attempts.

Mansa was a beautiful woman by any standards and Ntiamoah adored her much to the sorrow and bitterness of Okyere, her former husband, who had had to endure disgrace and mockery as each day passed. Ever since he placed a bet on his wife and son and lost them to Ntiamoah, everybody in and around Akyem called him 'The Fool'. People who heard the story came from far only to see him and go back. Even children played with his mishap. Gradually, the once sober Okyere took to drinking 'apio'; a hard liquor brewed from fermented palm wine. He began wasting away as the days turned into weeks and weeks into months. Silently, the chief had vowed to avenge his brother's demise. He called Mansa one night and tasked her with finding the meaning of Ntiamoah's haircut from him, and that he would reward her greatly with jewellery and beads from faraway lands. Mansa was not comfortable with the task but the lure of wealth and fame gradually sank into her mind. She would prepare Ntiamoah's favourite dish and would bathe and adorn herself with sweet smelling fragrance and sit by Ntiamoah while he ate. Night after night, she would lie on him and pester him to prove his love to her by telling her the answer to his riddle. Each night, Ntiamoah promised to tell her 'tomorrow'. Before long, Mansa realised 'tomorrow' was not a day that would come so with more craftiness, she lured Ntiamoah into swearing to tell her the meaning of the riddle on the evening before the final day of the riddle. The night finally came and Ntiamoah so soaked with love and desire for Mansa gave in.

The final evening came. The whole village gathered, ready to hear Ntiamoah display his wisdom one more time. Ntiamoah dressed in one of his most elaborate pieces of cloth walked majestically to the village square followed by his close friends. As was always the case, he stood in the middle and called out once more if anyone alive was wise enough to dig up the meaning of his riddle. He cast one final glance at the awed crowd and was just about to make his pronunciation when Okyere "The Fool" spoke up. He walked toward Ntiamoah and said with much calm and utter coldness:

"the first one on your forehead means "*wo nya asem a enka nkyere wo yere* mpo" (if you have an secret never tell your wife) and the second one means "*abanoma nsen oba pa*" (a stepson is not the same as a biological son)". The meaning of the third one is "*aniwa nnim awereho*" (tired eyes know no sorrow).

Ntiamoah was stunned. His eyes widened in horror as his hands spontaneously went to his head. How could this happen to him. The crowd let out a cheer as Okyere was carried shoulder high. Ntiamoah asked to be given three days to produce the morsel of gold.

Three days had passed, Ntiamoah could not produce the morsel of gold he promised. Okyere had asked for Ntiamoah's head if he was unable to fulfil the promise of gold. Ntiamoah had sold all his pieces of cloth, his beads, and everything he owned and yet, there he was sitting on the ground in the middle of the large gathering wearing nothing but a piece of tattered cloth that belonged to Mansa. The chief in the midst of his elders spoke through the linguist. He asked Ntiamoah if he had one last thing to say before he was led off to face the executioner. Just then, Mansa's son, Ntiamoah's stepson, rushed through the crowd and retrieved his mother's tattered cloth from Ntiamoah. Ntiamoah sat naked. He opened his mouth, tears began to flow from his eyes. He told the crowd that in actual fact, he was not lying when he said he had the gold he promised. He had, wrapped it in cloth and hidden it in a hole in the forest but when he went to pick it for Okyere, it was gone.

In the middle of the eager crowd, stood a stranger whose heart missed a beat at the hearing of Ntiamoah's final statement. That stranger was Osei! The lump of gold wrapped in the dirty cloth was for Ntiamoah! Two things tore into Osei's mind. Should he leave quietly like he was never there or he should own up and save the poor man's life. Afterall the gold was a 'gift' from the grasscutter. To give or not to give back? Integrity.

"Ntiamoah!" Osei shouted from within the crowd. All of a sudden there was utter silence. The crowd parted to give way to Osei.

"Here is your lump of gold. It found its way to me."

Ntiamoah took the piece of gold and there and then, it was weighed and given to Okyere, who kept grinding his teeth. All the same he felt he had redeemed his image. The crowd departed from the village square and reformed in groups of two and three discussing the interesting turn of events and who the stranger was. Meanwhile the chief impressed by Osei's honesty and integrity summoned him to his palace and inquired of him where he was from and what he wanted in their village. After Osei told him he was from Denkyira, the chief declined to harbour him in his village since Denkyira emissaries roamed that part of the land. He gave him water and food and made a guard escort him out of the village to continue his journey eastwards where he would find peace with a fetish priest of Asante origin who was a friend to the Chief.

As for Ntiamoah, he swore never to sleep a wink that night for his close shave with death but alas, worn out from the trauma he went through that day, he dozed off, slumped in a lazy chair. In fact, he even gained more respect because all three of his wise sayings that nearly had him killed came to pass. He secluded himself for months on end avoiding even his friends and family.

Chapter 11

O sei had walked the whole night. He had battled scorpions that had crawled on him when he sat to rest a little, and little poisonous snakes. In one hand, he held a young deer; the bow and arrow slung on his right shoulder, the sword in the other hand. Everyone he met assumed he was a hunter and greeted him with the welcoming greeting given to all successful hunters. He calmly responded with a nod and a smile, not sure whether the response in Bantama was the same here in these Akyem villages. When the sun was up, he sold the meat for a bowl of *ampesi* (boiled yam and stew). He didn't talk much and the times that he was forced to talk, he tried to copy the Denkyira ascent that he had learnt in the palace. He assumed he was doing well because none of the people he spoke to showed any surprise. He just kept on walking toward the rising sun. He didn't want to return to Asante because a search party would be sent to find him there. He was warmly greeted in all the villages through which he passed and children who saw him sang his praises. In those days, hunters were much respected for their bravery. It took a lot of courage to be in the forest at night alone at times, finding game. Stories had been coined around great hunters who killed leopards and lions and elephants. He himself had never come across any of those huge animals before although he had always dreamt of them. He had only seen a buffalo killed by the chief hunter in Bantama when he was seventeen years old. It was as large as the cattle from the northern states but with fearsome horns and eyes. The head and skin of the buffalo was sent to the king of Bantama as a souvenir and the meat shared among the families of Bantama. That day, the hunter became a living legend. His family walked in the village proudly all the days after. After walking three days and three nights, he crossed the boundary from Denkyira into an unknown state. A small river signified the boundary. On one bank was the symbol of Denkyira state and on the other, the symbol of another state. He took a long needed bath in the river and continued walking east. He still kept killing game and posing as an ordinary hunter who had strayed into unknown territory. When he was hungry without any villages in sight, he would camp in any open space under large trees after assuring himself the area was free from soldier ants and other harmful insects and reptiles. He would make a fire with dried leaves and stones and roast part of the game he caught. He would eat and rest thinking about his home, his friends and his love. He would laugh about the good times he had had and weep a little about the mess from which he had ran away. He only wished he had exercised a little more control over his emotions. There were nights he dreamt seeing a woman clad in white cloth offering him a stool- a stool made entirely of gold. And this particular dream kept coming night after night. After walking for a week, he had grown so weary and his footwear was so worn out that he was more or less walking barefooted. Water was nowhere to be found. His throat was completely dry and the sun was mercilessly hot. Yet he trekked on. The little hope of finding a new home kept burning and keeping him alive. He knew he wouldn't be alive if he couldn't find water for another day. His pace was slower now because his feet were covered with blisters and every step came with renewed pain at his feet. His skin was drenched with sweat and so much dirt that his dark brown complexion was now completely black.

Chapter 12

A Young man lay in the dust, with blood dripping slowly from a deep cut above his eyebrow and right cheek. His ankle was also swelling by the minute, and the pain was unbearable. His name was Kodua. A few hours before, he was on his way back to his master's village with chicken, farm produce, beautiful beads and a small sack of cowries. Little did he know he would be made to bite the dust that afternoon. As he made his way through a deserted ravine, three pairs of eyes followed him for a while until when it was clear he was alone, the three robbers jumped from behind the thickets and overpowered him. Since Kodua was determined not to let go of his possessions without a fight, he ended up bloodied and left to bleed to death. Not too long after, a farmer chanced upon him lying in the dust and moaning. The farmer drew closer and upon seeing that Kodua looked like he was beaten by robbers, he took to his heels without a second thought. As a hunter approached, Kodua gasped with all the strength he could muster.

"Help!" "I'm dying." The hunter drew near, paused for a while and concluded that since he had a long journey to make before reaching his village, Kodua would be an additional burden. He retraced his steps and walked away without as much as a glance back at the unfortunate fellow. The day dragged on, the ground where he lay was now soaked with his own sweat and blood. He felt so weak he could barely lift an arm or turn his head. His vision was becoming blurred from losing much blood. He heard footsteps coming towards him, slowly he opened his blurry eyes to see a pair of large feet, "like those of an Asante man" right before him. The feet belonged to an already tired Osei Tutu. Osei Tutu felt pity for the poor young man who would be about his own age. With renewed energy from nowhere, Osei poured water over his wounds and tied them up with leaves. He propped Kodua's head against the root of a large tree and made him drink some water. Thoughts of the days he had spent with the herbalist in Denkyira came to him, and he felt he needed to extend the same care and attention to this young man as was done to save his life when he was stabbed. He glanced down at his ribs and saw the scar. He felt he could almost see Ama squatting close and caring for him.

"aw...aw." Another moan from Kodua made Osei snap from his daydream. He cut sticks of bamboo and tied them together to form a grid, then he wove leaves over it. He tied Kodua over the grid and strung one side over his shoulders with climbing plants. Slowly he took his steps as he dragged his new found friend through the ravine along the path.

Slowly, the herbs Osei applied to Kodua's wounds appeared to be working magic. He gained consciousness and they began to talk. It had been twelve nights and eleven days after Osei escaped from Denkyira palace. He followed the advice of Kodua who seemed to know the way to his village even though he was not fully fit. They walked for days until they came across a small village. Kodua signalled to Osei that he had reached his village.

As he neared the huts, he noticed that they were entering a shrine. They slowly entered through the front gate into the courtyard. An assistant appeared from one of the huts and helped carry an already weary Kodua into one of the huts. He signaled to Osei to remove his footwear at the entrance to the yard. He obeyed after which he was offered a seat. When Osei was asked what his mission was, he started talking in Asante, hoping it would make some sense to the fetish. He had come from far to seek the help of the fetish about a particular dream haunting him, on the way, he met Kodua at the brink of death and brought him home. The assistant responded in Asante, bringing relief to Osei. He went to knock on another door. He entered and ushered into the courtyard a fetish priest with long hair worn in dreadlocks and white clay smeared all over his face and body. The priest wore trinkets on his ankles and wrists and held a mysterious looking scepter in his left hand. He took his seat on an animal skin spread at one end of the court. The assistant relayed Osei's mission to him. He looked at Osei so hard with eyes that seemed so piercing that Osei felt uneasy. Then he asked Osei again where exactly in Asante he was coming from. When Osei replied that he was coming from Bantama, the fetish priest asked whether he was really from Bantama and not a native of Adum. He advised Osei to tell him the truth because he had also been having visions related to Osei's dream. It was then that Osei informed him that his mother was a native of Adum. The fetish asked him what his mother's name was, to which Osei replied. Upon hearing the name of Yaa Mansa Badua, the fetish got up from the skin, looked towards the sky with both arms raised. He chanted praises to

Otweduampon Nyankopon (Almighty God) and the spirit of Yaa Badua. He came closer to Osei Tutu and held his hands .

"Welcome to my abode, my young friend. For so many years I have waited for this day. My name used to be Kusi, but now I am Okomfo Anokye. The fifty-first messenger of the gods of Asante." Kodua, Okomfo Anokye's assistant gave him a calabash full of water. Osei Tutu gulped down the water like his very life flowed in it. He was shown a stream nearby to to go and have a bath. After being fully refreshed, he joined Okomfo Anokye and Kodua by the courtyard fire. Okomfo welcomed him again and then went on to narrate to his assistant and Osei Tutu how he came to his present state.

"I was born with the gift of seeing beyond the ordinary physical life. A fetish priest I met once told me I would be one, but I tried to run away from my destiny by living as a hunter in Adum village, in Asante. When I was a boy, I almost killed myself because I thought I was being haunted by my gift. Sometimes when I woke up in the night, I would be hearing strange conversations going on around the village even though I lay in my hut. And the conversations were as scary as you could imagine. I heard voices I later got to know as witches fighting over relatives and flesh. Sometimes too, I would have strange dreams in which I would see people I knew change into other animals and birds. As I grew up, I learnt how to manage and control my gift more and more. When I was eighteen years old, I fell in love with a young sixteen year old beauty who lived in the village. She was all a man could ever want in a wife. In addition, she had this sweet voice I could never erase from my mind. I used to hide from my family the best part of the meat I killed so that I could give her gifts of bush meat. She would be so delighted and prepare a very nice '*mpusuo*'(traditional soup). We would arrange to meet in a palm-hut I had built on the outskirts of the village. We would eat and drink sweet palm wine and share so much joy. I knew I was going to marry her until the unexpected happened months before the day we had agreed to inform our families." At this point, tears were beginning to fill his eyes. Osei listened with rapt attention hoping to unwrap the mystery surrounding him.

"The king sent a scout to find him a new wife. My bride-to-be was taken away from me. Even then we decided to remain friends. We became nice friends until the King's first wife and the chief priest set a trap for us. Yaa Mansa was cruelly sent as a sacrifice to the gods in the *Musuo Forest*. I knew the gods would reject the sacrifice of Yaa Mansa because she was innocent of the charges held against her and so did the chief priest of Adum. So I kept watch over her from a distance when she was tied up and left in the forest, lest the chief priest attempted to harm her himself. True to my fears, under the cover of darkness, I saw him going into the forest with a dagger. Fortunately, I had removed Yaa Mansa from under the Odum tree and hidden her in a cave in the forest. He would have murdered her and no one would have suspected it." He paused with a sad look on his face.

"So what happened next?" Osei asked.

"I knew the king's guards would be hunting me down so I had to run away." Okomfo replied.

"Why didn't you take her with you?" Osei asked again.

"I didn't have a good idea of where exactly I was going or what harm I was going to face so I couldn't ensure her safety with me. More over, she had fainted and I couldn't go far with her on my shoulder."

"So what did you do with her?" His assistant asked, lost in the story he was hearing. Okomfo gave him a look that seemed to remind him of his place.

"I carried her through the forest to Bantama and placed her on the path to one Opanin Asamoah's farm. I knew him to be a hospitable man. Then I ran. I ran through the forest, I ran for many days and many nights and finally settled here."

"Welcome, Osei Tutu, son of my love, the appointed one. Night after night, I have had visions of my love and the noble ancestors placing you on the golden stool."

"Are you saying that my father is the king of Adum? Osei Tutu asked.

"Yes, but have patience, my young friend and stay here with me. When the time is right and the seasons announce the will of the gods, you will certainly know."

Osei Tutu couldn't believe his ears. That the young man who threw him into slavery was his own half-brother. Nobody had told him that secret in his life all this while and he would never have known if he hadn't been pushed into making this journey. The destiny of a man surely has one strange way of revealing itself. Osei Tutu in turn told Okomfo Anokye all that had happened exactly. Right from Papa Bonsu, telling him how he found his mother down to how he appeared in Akwamu land. So Osei had come to meet the love of his mother. The man accused of committing adultery with his mother. Finally the mystery over how his mother was found unconscious on a farm path had been revealed. He settled down in his new found home awaiting what destiny had in store for him next.

Chapter 13

Three years and six moons had passed. Ama had conceived the night she spent with Osei in her room. As a result, her suitor refused to marry her, much to her delight. The moment she fell in love with Osei, she knew she was never going to get married because there was no way her family was going to allow her, a royal to marry an Asante slave and she was also not ready to marry anyone apart from Osei, her first love. Though under normal circumstances, she should have been disowned by her kinsmen, nobody was bold enough to do that because of her unusual wisdom and courage. She openly criticized the tradition of looking down on people from other tribes and preventing people from marrying their loved ones because of tribal differences. In addition to that, she spoke in public against slavery and won the admiration of many of the respected people in Fosu. At gatherings of elders, she would organize sections of the youth and they would express the social harm that these traditions pose. Ama pursued what she believed in and with time, she came to win the respect of the youth and elderly in Fosu. When a new king was enstooled, she became the envoy of the king of Denkyira. She was sent to negotiate alliances and peace with other states on behalf of Denkyira. Her son was named Adu Bempah by her maternal uncle who stood by her when she was being scorned for causing an abomination. The child looked very much like Osei Tutu and even as he grew up without knowing Osei as his father, he exhibited traits that were very much like Osei Tutu. In as much as these brought joy on Ama's face, it never ceased to infuriate her other kinsmen who felt she had disappointed them. At times when she felt she couldn't take the scorn any longer, she would still hold a bold face and find a quiet place where she could be alone and let out all the tears and hate she was experiencing. She would cry for hours till her tears became like water and lost the salty taste. When she felt she had had enough, she would return to her room feeling much better.

Back in Adum, Kojo Akenten, the Deliverer, had become so powerful. Because he had been taught all the customs and laws, he had found ways of manipulating them to his advantage. Even though as the son of the sitting Asante chief, he was never in line to ascend the throne, he schemed to make himself next in line. He could order for whatever he wanted from whomever he wished. He was the most feared person in Adum aside the king even though under normal circumstances it shouldn't have been so. Instead of building his army, he was rather imprisoning more and more of the men. He threw into prison and subsequently into slavery anyone who refused to obey him or spoke against him. Almost everybody in Adum knew by then that Kojo Akenten was a coward. He couldn't even fire an arrow straight much less a spear. He tried to use power to cover his shortfalls and that seem to be working for him although for a short time. He was wise enough to know sooner than later, he would have to show whether he was the Deliverer. He spent days with the chief priest. He wanted him to make him more powerful. The chief priest made all the charms that he knew would make a man powerful for him. In a particular year, he was wearing as many as ten charms on his body: three around his neck, two around his waist, one round his ankles, one on his wrist and three as rings on his fingers. Even these did not give him the courage that he needed to be a warrior much less lead an army. "Courage is never bought. It is nurtured and developed from believing in what you do and the course you ply." A wise man he consulted once told him. Of course, that 'insulting' wise man was thrown into prison for an orchestrated offence.

Meanwhile, Denkyira was tormenting the Asante states with severe oppression. The tributes to be paid to Denkyira were increased dramatically and they began to establish forts in the Asante villages where they would appoint representatives with a number of guards to live permanently on Asante soil. These were causing a lot of unrest on the Asante villages but they could not stand up to the might of Denkyira because they were not united and had no standing army. Their 'Deliverer' had turned out to be a tyrant to his own people. He sent the strong who could stand against him as slaves to Denkyira year after year.

Chapter 14

Finally, the time was right. Osei, having learned all about spiritual and natural secrets from Okomfo Anokye, led the group of three to put things right where they belonged in Asante. They had come to the decision to finally return from having series and series of repetitive dreams. Dreams of Asantes crying out their names. Osei had missed Bonsu, his Papa, so much and wished to look into his eyes again. He had never seen him for seven whole years. They set off at dawn on a Thursday after a sacrifice of a hen and prayers by Okomfo Anokye. Each had a knapsack with a few belongings inside and a sword in his waist belt. In addition, Osei carried his bow and arrow on his shoulder. Kodua, who had also spent the past years in the shrine decided to go with them because he owed Osei for saving his life. To avoid any confrontations, they went round Denkyira state instead of passing through it. The journey back seemed shorter than before even though the way was longer. They reached Bantama in the cool of the evening. There had been marked difference in the village. Osei's heart was beating fast at the thought of seeing his

Papa again after so long a time. They passed the Denkyira fort in Bantama as Osei watched the men with a lot of caution. He reasoned that it would be quite difficult to identify him. He run away from Denkyira when he was about twenty-two years old and now, he was almost twenty-eight with beard on his face. Kodua remarked that Bantama was indeed a very neat and beautiful village, to which they both agreed. As they rounded the bend, Osei was expecting to see his home and probably some of his brothers and sisters but they found to their dismay, a horror! There were no buildings and no souls, instead, overgrown weeds and pieces of burnt out wood and bricks! Osei stood there shaking as Okomfo tried to reason out with him that they might have missed the direction to his home. They saw a woman going towards the village with water in an earthen ware pot. They called her and Okomfo Anokye asked:

"Woman, we are from far away and we have been sent to give a message to one Bonsu the farmer. Where can we locate his house?"

"Bonsu? Son of Opanin Asamoah?" the woman asked. Osei answered yes.

"Oh! Haven't you been told? He was killed by the Denkyira-hene about two years ago along with all his family. They claimed he was hiding a man accused of murdering Denkyira royals. They burnt down his house as well." Upon hearing this, Osei Tutu fell on his knees in the burnt soil. He wept so loudly, the woman couldn't help but wonder why? Okomfo Anokye asked whether the woman knew where they were buried to which the woman informed them that the men in the fort took their bodies and buried them at an undisclosed location. He thanked the woman and tried lifting Osei up from the ground. Osei's whole body was vibrating with the shock of being the cause of the death of the greatest man he had ever known and all his brothers, sisters and even his foster mother. It was almost dark. He got up on his feet, eyes red like a wounded tiger. He armed himself with his sword, bow in hand and arrows slung on his left shoulder. Okomfo held him by the shoulders and looked straight into his eyes.

"Now is the right time for your anger!" Then his Papa's words came back to him. "To be angry is easy. But to be angry at the right person, at the right time, for the right reason, that is difficult." They left their knapsacks in the care of Kodua and run towards the fort. After careful planning, they attacked the men in the fort from opposite directions. Overpowering them was swift and easy because the guards in the fort were totally unaware of what was lurking in the darkness for them. After killing all the twelve guards in the fort, they set it ablaze. The fire drew the people of the village out of their houses. Osei Tutu and Okomfo Anokye stood in the middle of the gathered crowd and introduced themselves and their reasons for burning down the fort. The people gasped when they heard the return of Osei Tutu. Osei spoke boldly to the people to resist the tyranny of Denkyira. He made them know they were strong enough to be a free people if they were united. Most of the people got incited although a few were still dreading the consequences. Osei asked the men who were aged between twenty years and sixty years to take up arms to defend their village against the new enemy, Denkyira.

Early the next morning, Osei Tutu upon the advice of Okomfo Anokye rallied all the men who were ready to fight for Bantama. They were mostly untrained in the art of war but with their determination, Osei knew they could defend their village for some time. They put the men in strategic positions so that any enemy would be seen from a far distance. By noon the next day, all the villages in Asante had heard about Osei Tutu and his daring deeds. Denkyira-hene sent an army of fifty men to crush the rebellion in Bantama village. The fifty men were trapped and locked up in a very intelligent and coordinated action. This boosted the morale of the men. They were now ready to shed their blood for their village. Osei Tutu sent an envoy to the Denkyirahene to stay off Bantama village and messages urging the other Asante villages to fight for their freedom. In three days, fifteen out of the eighteen Asante villages had thrown the Denkyira guards out of their villages and were proclaiming independence. The only villages that were still fully under the control of Denkyira were Adum, Amakom and Asokwa.

In Adum, it had happened that Kojo Akenten's mother had been struck by a strange disease for more than two years. She had been sent to all the herbalists and fetish priests in Asante yet no cure had been found for her strange sickness. Okomfo Anokye heard of her disease and quickly planned a way to expose the truth that had long been hidden. He made Kodua disguise himself as a soothsayer. Kodua went to her house where she was in bed and started talking about prophesies and the fact that he knew of a fetish priest who had the gift of healing. Quickly an arrangement was made by the family of Kojo's mother to send her along for healing. When she was brought before Okomfo Anokye, Okomfo started invoking oracles and chanting. He made known to all around that Kojo's mother had a confession to make. Initially, she tried to deny it but Okomfo warned her that if she lied, she would surely die. For fear of death, Kojo's mother confessed to all gathered that Yaa Mansa Badua was innocent of the charges brought on her. And that it was out of jealousy that she schemed with the then chief priest. Okomfo Anokye sent her back without healing her because the sickness was a curse from the gods as a result of her evil deeds. That evening, Okomfo Anokye wept for the memory of his love, Yaa Mansa. One thing he was glad about was that he had stood up and brought the person responsible for her banishment to book. Before then, he had always blamed himself for letting a crime like that go unpunished when he knew the truth. The confession spread like wild fire. It brought much contempt on Kojo Akenten and the whole family. All the villages of Asante got to hear of the terrible deed of Otumfuo Oti Akenten's first wife. The rest of her days were spent in much sorrow.

Chapter  15

Ama Birago, sat in a porch in the royal palace in Denkyira eating avocado. She could not help but admire the courage in the Asante man who had killed a fort full of guards to avenge the death of his family. How she wished she could at least see him with her own two eyes. The report from her maid was that this strange man was as big as three men put together and as tall as two average height men. In all her life, she had known one man who was almost as brave although not as gigantic as was being peddled around. Osei Tutu. Unfortunately, that man was alleged to have been killed as he was trying to escape from Denkyira after killing two guards. That was the report given in Denkyira by the guards who were sent to recapture Osei Tutu, when he escaped. Though his dead body was never seen, everyone in Fosu knew Osei had been killed. Ama had mourned him for days and yet the memory of him was still fresh in her mind. Sometimes she would call out his name in her sleep. At a point in time she wished for death so she could go and meet her love in 'Asamando'(the land of the dead). She picked up what was remaining of the fruit and walked to her mother's house to feed her naughty son before he gave his grandmother any troubles.

Back in Adum, Kojo Akenten paced up and down in the throne room. He just could not believe that out of thin air, the people were making a legend of an Osei Tutu in Bantama. Who was he? Was he going to take his authority as the Deliverer from him? Kojo had worked his way to the throne of Adum after the death of Otumfuo Oti Akenten, even though he was not the next in line to be made a king. He manipulated the laws of the land to his favour. In addition, he was able to bribe some of the members of the council of elders. He now ruled with fear in his eyes because he was very much aware that the people were fed up with his oppression and were running out of patience waiting for him to lead them against Denkyira, the tyrant. For so many years they waited for the birth of the Deliverer. When Kojo was born, supposedly as the first son of the Otumfuo, they had to wait for some more years for him to mature and lead them. After waiting for Kojo to become a man, there seem to be still no sign of him waking up to his duty and his destiny. All the labour of their hands went into supporting the royal family and as tributes to Denkyira. Not only those, their sons and sometimes daughters, brothers and sisters and even fathers were taken away from them into slavery in Denkyira. Now there was a new wave blowing over all the villages in Asante. A new legend had suddenly appeared. Osei Tutu and his friend Okomfo Anokye, were rallying through the villages with a large following of men volunteering to join the new Asante army. Even though Osei was still young, his new found determination inspired the men. Okomfo Anokye advised him on how best to lead the men and win their hearts. It had come to a time when the men respected Osei Tutu more than even their village chiefs.

Chapter 16

O sei Tutu!" The name struck Ama Birago like lightening.
"Are you sure this leader is Osei Tutu?" She asked again.
Filled with a mixture of fear, anxiety and some joy.
"Yes, your honour." Replied her aid.

Ama stood up from her seat in the palace.

"You may leave now." She told her aide. Alone in the large room where the advisors to the throne met, she let go of her tears as the streams flowed gently down her beautiful cheeks. She knew there was something special about Osei Tutu the moment she saw him unconscious after being stabbed. Now, he had almost delivered Asante from Denkyira. There was a lot of confusion in several quarters in Denkyira as a result of one man, the man she loved. She paced up and down thinking about how to approach a very dreaded enemy who also happened to be the love of her life. Finally, she reached a decision.

Osei Tutu was with Okomfo Anokye in the house given to them in Bantama. There was a knock on the door and a guard informed them that there was an envoy with a message from the

Denkyirahene. He left Okomfo Anokye, his advisor and went out to receive the message from the envoy. A tent had been erected for the envoy just outside Osei Tutu's house. Osei Tutu, passed the guards at the entrance to the tent and entered. The envoy was seated on a stool, head bowed with a veil covering the face and two servants standing around. Osei could not see the face but he reasoned the envoy was a woman from the sweet-smelling perfume in the tent and the servants being girls.

"What news do you bring from Denkyira?" he asked.

She asked the servants to leave the tent. Slowly, she got up from her seat, and lifted her tear-filled eyes.

"Ama."

"Osei"

He hugged her trembling body tight as more tears flowed. They sat down and at first, they were both confused not knowing what to do or say. She told Osei all that had happened since he left Denkyira. The scorn she had to go through and the fact that they had a son. Osei couldn't believe his ears. He had been a father all that while. He hugged her more and shared all that he had gone through with her and the fact that he nearly perished before reaching Akwamu. Then it got to the message she had been sent to deliver. The wise men of Denkyira had long known that when united, Asante would be as large and mighty as Denkyira itself so they had buried this truth and tried as best as they could to keep Asante disunited. They were now troubled by the news that a man had risen in Asante who was succeeding in bringing all the villages together. Their request was to ask Osei Tutu to come to Fosu to swear an oath that Asante would no longer pay tributes to Denkyira but would also not attack Denkyira. Osei Tutu tried to let Ama understand that the only way to ensure peace between

Denkyira and Asante was for Denkyira to be defeated. There they were, two lovers on the opposite sides of the devide. Ama could not allow her own people to suffer defeat. He led her into the house to meet Okomfo Anokye and Kodua. The four of them sat down and deliberated on what to do. Ama tried as best as she could to dissuade them from going to war with her people. When it was getting late, she asked to leave. Okomfo Anokye didn't agree with Osei Tutu going to Denkyira to swear the peace treaty. He knew there was a hidden agenda. Osei on the other hand didn't see any harm that Denkyira could do to him. After deliberating the whole night, Okomfo Anokye suggested that they consult the gods. After consulting the gods, they reached a compromise. Early the next morning, four guards accompanied Osei Tutu and they set off for Fosu, the capital of Denkyira state.

Ama Birago was quite a worried woman. There seemed to be something fishy going on that she didn't understand. She had the feeling word had gone out that the slave who killed two royal guards and ran away from Denkyira some years back was the new leader of the Asantes. She knew if the king got to know of it, Osei Tutu would surely not leave Denkyira alive. She made up her mind to go and find out if the King had any hint of it so she could forewarn Osei Tutu. As she got nearer the throne room, she heard two voices she knew very well, the King of Denkyira and the Chief in charge of the defense guards.

"Was the woman able to convince him?"

"Yes, my lord."

"What time will the Asante be arriving?"

"At noon, my lord."

"Hope you had the instructions on what to do."

"Yes, my lord."

"Remember, if this Asante leaves here alive, that would be the end of the Denkyira Empire."

Ama Birago gasped at the realization. She had been used as a bait to trap Osei. She spun round to find a giant of a man towering over her. He was a chief warrior in the Denkyira army. He dragged Ama inside and told the king he had found her eavesdropping. He was ordered to lock her up. Ama screamed and fought as she was dragged to an inner room in the palace. She was desperate. The death of Osei would be the worst thing to ever happen to her. She now knew that her love for Osei Tutu was more powerful than her love for her state.

The five men from Asante entered Fosu from the north. Everybody who saw them stopped whatever they were doing to look at them. As soon as they reached the palace grounds, guards pounced on them and slew them. They cut off the head of the leader of the group and went to present it to the Denkyira hene. The king put the head on the ground and stepped on it, signifying his triumph over his enemy. When word went round that Osei Tutu had been killed, there was great rejoicing in Denkyira. Ama cried so much that she feared she might not live to see the next day. She refused food the whole day even after she was released.

After waiting for six hours without the return of the group they sent to sign the peace treaty, Okomfo Anokye and Osei Tutu concluded that the message borne by Ama was a ploy to kill him. Osei Tutu couldn't believe it, that the woman who had sworn love to him could plot to kill him. Okomfo Anokye after consulting the gods had suggested that they find someone who looked like Osei Tutu. They did and sent him at the head of the delegation to Fosu as if it was Osei Tutu himself. He sent word to all the warriors who had been appointed over sections of the new army. They were to fight for their total freedom from Denkyira at dawn the next day. Before then, they had an important internal matter to take care of.

Chapter 17

Kojo Akenten sat reclining in his resting chair after the evening meal. He was hoping that Denkyira would crush the rebellion in Bantama so that there would be no one to challenge his kingship. Suddenly he heard loud voices of men chanting war songs. He belched. He asked a servant to find out and report to him what was going on. Before the servant could return, the group had burst into the palace and there was no where for him to escape to. Four men lifted him shoulder high as his own guards stood by. He shouted for them to rescue him but they even opened the door for the men carrying him to descend down into the courtyard. They dropped him at the feet of two men standing in the middle of the guards. One was an Okomfo and he drew the conclusion that the other must be Osei Tutu. By the motion of his right hand, two of the guards immediately removed Kojo Akenten's sandals and slapped his head with them signifying the end of his kingship. Osei looked at him with anger.

"Moron, tie him up and bring him along!" Osei ordered, using the very words that years before, Kojo had used to turn him into a slave. As the group of men left the palace and into the streets of Adum, chanting patriotic songs, someone shouted from the crowd, " Behold the Deliverer of Asante!" then they all responded in a loud cheer, "Deliverer! Deliverer! Deliverer!...." Kojo could not believe his ears. Osei Tutu being referred to as the Deliverer! At the village square, the gong was beaten and all the people in Adum gathered. Many had heard of the name Osei Tutu but had not seen him before. Many were those who had rumored him to be a huge giant. He raised his arms with his hand clenched in a fist and shouted out to the people.

"My name is Osei Tutu. First son of Otumfuo Oti Akenten and Yaa Mansa Badua!" Most of the people were astonished to hear that Kojo Akenten was not the first son as everyone in Adum had been deceived into believing. Kojo himself never knew. He suddenly burst into tears as he trembled at the thought of being thrown into slavery. Suddenly a wry old voice that seemed all too familiar to Osei screamed from somewhere within the crowd!

"When you are born to kill an elephant, you don't go bruising your knees chasing rats!"

Osei Tutu froze then looked harder into the crowd. The cheering crowd became quiet and followed his gaze as he parted the people and faced the strange old man with no arms whom he met years ago. Only this time, he was with arms and hands and holding onto an old staff.

"Why? Are you surprised? Youngman?" He asked.

"No. I only wanted to thank you for your lesson." Osei replied

"You were pre-destined for today. Go now and lead your people and remember that not everyone you see around is flesh and blood. Some of us were sent to your world to guide you. Remember the grasscutter on which you had mercy . That was your test of kindness. Remember Ntiamoah's gold, that was your test of integrity. Remember Kodua in a pool of blood, that was your test of empathy" He whispered and walked away.

For a moment, Osei stood rooted to the spot. He then turned to the teaming crowd and shouted! "Tsooooo bui!"

The people responded "Yei!'

"Tsooooooooooooo bui!"

"Yeeeeeeeeeeeei!"

"I have come firstly to unite you and to lead you to gain your freedom. Though the prophecy referred to me, the Deliverer is not I, but each one of you gathered here, if you would love Asante more and offer to fight for her tomorrow against her oppressors. Mother Asante calls on you. Draw your swords, lift your spears and fight for her!" All the people cheered in a loud voice. Someone shouted again "Deliverer!" then the chant was on. "Deliverer! Deliverer! Deliverer!......" The women threw rotten tomatoes and vegetables at Kojo Akenten as he was being escorted through the streets of all the Asante villages. It had come to light that during the two years that he had ascended the throne of Adum, he had sold more men and women into slavery than ever before. He was driven away from the palace to spend the rest of his life in a hut on the outskirts of Adum. He was stripped of all his servants and concubines. Since he could neither hunt nor farm, he started growing leaner by the day. Finally, he ended up as a begger who travelled from village to village.

The next day, Osei Tutu, led a united Asante in the fight for freedom against the mighty Denkyira. For three years they fought in the hills and plains, dry seasons and wet seasons. At the beginning of the war, the Denkyira army outnumbered the Asantes by three men to two. The might of Denkyira was overwhelming but the Asantes fought with determination and courage. Though he had virtually no experience in warfare, Osei Tutu led the men skillfully. He put into practice what he had learnt from the prince of Denkyira years before. Okomfo Anokye fought the spiritual battles and inspired the people. Each evening, Ama Birago stood on the balcony of the Denkyira palace and watched as the chief warriors and the generals brought reports from the battle front to the king. She was torn between her love for Denkyira and Osei Tutu. She only wished she could have both without bloodshed. When she walked through the streets of Fosu, she wept when she heard mothers wailing for their sons and husbands who had perished. How long must this avoidable war continue? She asked herself time and time again. After the fourth straight year of fighting, Ama Birago couldn't take the bloodshed any longer. She knew she had to do something. She had to end the war even if it meant betraying her state; at least, she would have saved hundreds of innocent sons and husbands. Meeting Osei Tutu again would spell doom for her but she knew she had to take the risk. Moreover, she couldn't predict the mood of Osei after she was used as bait to trap him.

"If only Osei knew the truth", she mused. After thinking deeply on how to meet Osei again, Ama found a way. She paid a visit to Adjei, the kente weaver who had remained in the room where he wove for so many years. Adjei listened carefully as she lamented on how she felt about the war and her plan for ending it. Adjei remained silent for so long a time that Ama began feeling irritated. He silently offered to help her. After all, his days were almost over. If they were killed in their quest for peace, so be it.

Chapter  18

They set off after disguising themselves as foreign peddlers. Avoiding the war front, they joined the trade routes and made their way to Asante and then to Bantama. They met Okomfo Anokye who after listening to them carefully assessed and accepted that Ama was innocent of the ploy to kill Osei Tutu. Osei was called from the battle front by a messenger. She made Osei Tutu promise her that he would not subject the Denkyira people to the same oppression that the Asantes had to go through. When he promised, she offered to show Osei Tutu the secret of the strength of Denkyira. She would do this to prove to Osei Tutu that she was innocent of the plot to kill him and to avenge the betrayal by her own king. She met Osei and Okomfo Anokye at an undisclosed location and told them the secret. The secret was that every midnight, the spirit of Denkyira state played a game of 'oware' and won against the spirit of another Denkyira royal who disguised himself as being the spirit of Asante state.

The game of 'oware' was sacred to the royals of Denkyira. Nobody knew the origin nor the creator of the game. It was played upon a wooden carving with twelve holes facing each player and one adjoining hole each. A set of forty-eight pebbles were traded round the holes in a particular order. *Oware* was exclusive to the wise and selected few in Denkyira. Until the spirit of a real Asante who knew how to play the *oware* played with that of Denkyira and won, Asante could never win the war against Denkyira. Since the oware was the sacred game of the Denkyira royal family, there was no Asante who knew how to play it. For all the years that Osei Tutu spent in the Denkyira palace, he heard mention of it only twice. Ama Birago taught Osei Tutu how to carve it, and then offered to sneak under the cover of darkness to Bantama to teach Okomfo Anokye how to play the *oware* for a whole year.

The year passed quickly. When Okomfo Anokye had fully learnt all the tricks in the game he still needed to do one more thing to achieve victory: a human sacrifice to the gods of the *oware* game. This was a very difficult time in Asante. Okomfo Anokye announced to the kings of the villages of Asante at a gathering one Wednesday evening that the key to winning the war was an Asante sacrifice. Three days passed with nobody owing up to be sacrificed for the cause of the Asante state. There was sorrow through out the whole land. Some of the kings were calling for Asante to surrender because they saw defeat was inevitable. Finally, Kodua, Okomfo Anokye's servant offered his head as a sacrifice for victory over Denkyira.

The Friday night on which Kodua was to be beheaded as a sacrifice for the victory of Asante eventually came. Asante had never seen a darker night. There was utter quietness throughout the land with occasional shrieks and a fiery howl of the eastern wind. That night, heavy clouds hung so low that the mist reached all the way to the ground. One could barely see his own nose much less his feet when he looked down. No one needed to be told to stay indoors. Mothers and daughters hugged closely in fear. Men trembled in silence, refusing to show any sign of fear in their bid to impress their women and children. Even the warriors clenched their teeth to prevent them from rattling as they held on to their spears. Suddenly there was the sound of mysterious drums. No one knew where the drums were being played. Okomfo Anokye appeared in the steets and danced through the night followed by the sound of the drums but with no drummers! As the drumming became louder, there was a sudden gush of wind from the west clashing with the howl from the east. A mighty whirlwind arose and Okomfo Anokye was lifted up into the spiritual realm. Suddenly the drumming ceased, there was silence. Yaa Mansa Badua's spirit met him in a breeze and led him to replace the disguised Denkyira player around the *oware*. None of the spirits present could recognize that they had been tricked because they were drunk with the blood of Kodua. The game began as the physical body of Okomfo Anokye was carried to rest in his room in Bantama. As they played in the spiritual realm, a sign appeard to Osei Tutu launch the attack against the Denkyiras in the physical realm. That night, the battles began in earnest. Denkyiras seemed to be winning the battle as their representative spirit was winning the game of oware over the spirit of Okomfo Anokye. Most of the Asantes were giving up already. The war with Denkyira had been too long and much more costly than they ever anticipated. That night, Osei Tutu kept inspiring them. Night after night, the battle raged on, each side determined to end the years of fighting with a victory. Then the tides turned, after fifteen nights of *oware*, Okomfo Anokye won his first victory. The next morning, the Asante state won a decisive battle which gingered them to press on. Okomfo Anokye won another victory, then another, then another. As Okomfo Anokye kept winning, Osei Tutu and his forces kept pursuing and slaying the Denkyira army. And so it happened that on the seventh day of the seventh moon of the fifth year after war was declared, the united Asante pursued the Denkyiras to the palace of Fosu where they went to find the mysterious golden *oware* being played in a secret room in the palace with no souls around but the pebbles moving by themselves!

Chapter 19

After six long years of war, Denkyira came to be a part of the Asante Empire. Osei Tutu was installed as the first and greatest king of united Asante at a Friday gathering. Okomfo Anokye, the powerful one, appeared at the gathering of the chiefs in a different state. He danced mysteriously to and fro. Suddenly, the sky turned dark and lightening began to flash. In the midst of the thundering, a stool made entirely of gold and adorned with eighteen bells, each signifying a particular Asante State right onto the lap of Osei Tutu. Osei could not believe his eyes. The same stool that had appeared in his dreams on the way to Akwamu. "This is to be the soul of the Asante state and must be protected at all cost", Okomfo Anokye pronounced. Osei Tutu was given the title, First Occupier of the Golden Stool. All the Asante slaves returned home to reunite with their families. Feeling sad about the sacrifice his family had made, Osei Tutu decided to visit the drum-maker and his sons. He got to the compound only to see his own brothers and sisters very much alive! The story was that when the warriors from Denkyira were sent to kill Papa Bonsu and his family, he managed to send the family to the drum-maker who hid them in huge fontomfrom drums and so they were able to escape with the exception of Bonsu who surrendered to save his family. A week was set aside to mourn the great father who lived and died so his family would lack nothing even though he was a poor farmer. All the subjects of the newly created Asante kingdom mourned for the soul of the departed Papa Bonsu. A few weeks after the funeral ceremony was complete, the wedding day came.

Osei Tutu married Ama Birago in a very colourful ceremony on the compound of the former Denkyira Palace which was also home to Ama. Early in the morning, young women from Asante carried head pans full of ornaments, garments, kente and jewelry to Denkyira as presents for Ama and her family as part of the marriage ceremony. Later in the day, Okomfo Anokye, led a large procession of all the chiefs in Asante and Osei Tutu to go and complete the marriage ceremony. It had turned into a grand durbar with chiefs carried high in palanquins by subjects. Ama had spent a greater part of the day being adorned with all the rare treasures from Denkyira and beyond. By midday, she could barely move from the weight of ornaments she wore beautifully on her ankles, waist, neck and wrists. Her skin shone from the beautiful red and white clay that had been smeared on her. Her hair was adorned with cowries from the north and seashells from further south. As she moved from her room to the palace durbar grounds in the mist of her entourage, drummers and horn blowers accompanied her with beautiful tunes. On the durbar grounds, she danced so beautifully with her aides. The marriage rites were performed and celebration began throughout the entire kingdom. The celebrations lasted a whole week. True to

Osei Tutu's promise to Ama, the Denkyira people were seen as Asantes and were not oppressed. Together with their son, Adu Bempah, they lived in a big palace in the town of Manhyia, the new capital of the Asante state.

Okomfo Anokye lived to a very old age and vanished one day never to be found again. Some said he went in search of an antidote for death. Others said he went to live with Yaa Mansa Badua, his love. Well, who knows, he might return one day. As for the golden stool, it has remained the soul of the Asante people kept in a secret room in the Asantehene's palace at Manhyia.

A few years after Osei Tutu began his reign as the king of the united Asante Kingdom, a new enemy arose from the south...